Charlie Nash was born in England and holds degrees in mechanical and space engineering, medicine, and writing. Her fiction has been shortlisted for the Aurealis and Ditmar awards. She lives on the eastern seaboard of Australia, and is working on two new novels, and a third Ship's Doctor installment.

 charlienash.net

f authorcharlienash

Also by Charlie Nash:

Men and Machines II:
punks and postapocalypticans

CHARLIE NASH

FLYING
— NUN —
PUBLICATIONS

Published in 2019 by Flying Nun Publications, http://flyingnunpublications.com/

"Blue ICE" first published 2014 in *Andromeda Spaceways Inflight Magazine #59*

"The Message" first published 2014 in *Dimension6 #1*

"Alchemy & Ice" first published 2015 in *Andromeda Spaceways Inflight Magazine #61*

"Arachne" published 2019 in *Men and Machines II: punks and postapocalypticans.*

In all the above first publications, stories originally credited to Charlotte Nash.

ISBN:
978-1-925775-11-2 (paperback)
978-1-925775-12-9 (eBook)

A catalogue record for this book is available from the National Library of Australia

Cover design by Richard Priestley

Contents

BLUE ICE

Tak knows a dozen words for grub, all of them cut with curses, and none these men will understand. She'll have to reach for something basic. There's *mud*, of course, but you don't get mud here under the artificial irrigators. Mud is from back home, where the filth flows with a kind of clean consistency. Sloshes in wheel ditches on old-style farms where you'd still find people in the machinery.

Yeah, well, at least you used to. Here in Dubai, Tak knows mud is only in salons. And you'll never find Tak in a salon.

Right now, she's knee deep in quicksand squelch, clip-pad shedding brown fluid, yelling at the men through the tumbling shit-water. Her ears are full of the stuff, and when she shouts, it runs between her teeth, coating her tongue with grit and sterilizer.

She spits. *Ugh.* Nothing but a sticky rice and a number twenty-three from *Hiro's* will cut the taste. But she's responsible for this pipe-farm fuck-up, the heart of the system that grows food on land that should be desert.

And somewhere high in the snaking, pipe-laden ceiling, the system has a constipated shit-jam.

Tak punches her commlink, holding the clip-pad umbrella fashion over her head. "*Mud,*" she gargles. "Look for mud!"

Crackling chatter. The men are overhead in the pipes looking for the blockage. The one that dried up the irrigators a half-k down the next field. It's a system quirk that the block happens right over where the rain's still working, and the flowing squelch water doesn't stop for anything, even for fault-finders making quagmire with next year's sorghum.

She falls over the squelching mud-pile before she sees it. Then the sucking mud is inside her collar, sticking her 'ralls to skin, tumbling down her legs. Her boots feel like quick-set cement, but she's got a rage going now, which means things are about to happen. The fault is right overhead.

Tak hauls out of the mud, zombie-style: hair straggling, mouth drawn, teeth bared white and rimmed in grime. She spies a stalk: one of the structural conduits that both hold the roof, and jam the harvest machines when their position sensors get coated in the mud. Tak's commlink isn't even giving static now: given up to the squelch. So she finds the stalk side, caving-ladder style, and hauls her ass up, along with two tons of mud.

Once she gets up above the crop heads, the ladder is a streaming slick. Tak wishes she had her GrippyFingers right now, but they're tucked in her apartment back home, wedged between the mattress and the bed-end. Finally, she reaches the zone above the spray and hauls her dripping 'ralls onto the pipe deck. Down the line, she sees the blue-covered shapes of men, and the thin wisps of vape-smoke rising roof-wards. *Lazy fuckers.*

She stomps her boots into the pipe trays, ready to rip them new sphincters, when the expanding mud-pile glops into view. There's the problem: a ball-valve control stick glows red: *off.* The pressure has pushed the mud line through the seals, shorting out the water line next door. Tak runs back up the line in irritation. Shouldn't fucking happen. There's a relief valve here that should blow first … then she finds it, its own control stick as red as the Webz Great Red Beyond. Nice. Someone's got the line on manual, and forgot to switch it back.

She throws the switch at the emergency panel and is back in the lockers in under five, mouth full of grit and curses. She calls it in while she stands under the sprays. Boss answers in a flat minute by busting in, unannounced, overriding locks like a tank across a kid's cardboard fort. Tak is lucky she's still in the 'ralls, because she could be buck naked right now. But she knows this about Boss, and she never gets naked at work.

"Manual mode fuck-up," she spits at him, shutting down preamble as she shuts down the water. "Some jerk in your software room's got his hand on it instead of watching the program."

Boss eyes her back with the searching up-and-down. His hair is a standing coif, wind-defying hair replacement. Tak knows it's real hair on the outside but synthetic core, just like Boss himself, and all of it standing proud of a barren body landscape; a body made for slouch and fueling the brain-center called management. Not what a body's made for.

"Right," he says, with such an inflection that Tak knows the aforementioned Jerk in Software's going to get reamed in precisely five minutes.

Then Boss narrows his eyes, so Tak sees the crinkle wave his eyelids put on the contact lenses. Tak wonders if he has transtex imagers in those lenses, and he's looking at her naked anyway, 'ralls stripped to just her skin and tatts. His smile veneers glitter like wet bone. "Get dry," he says. "Scram's off the pad in forty-five. New problem for you in Sydney."

Boss leaves a trail of sour deodorant-cloaked man-stink, or maybe that's just Tak's brain remembering Sydney. Olfactory is the most primitive sense, just a step below the one she uses to understand what Boss really means: *Good job; you can keep it another week.*

The Scram busts through the curve of the Earth, and East Coast Australia expands in the forward camera view. In the ten-inch, seat-inlayed screen, Tak watches the light cluster explode into starfield. Sydney is a glowing nebula, webby fingers spreading inland. But north of the border is a new, dark patch. Where Brisbane used to be. No lights, no nothing there. A wasteland, now, flooded and destroyed, and she can't get used to that.

Off the Scram, her transport shoots through the tunnels, ejecting her into the basement office of her MegaCorp employer. She stands impatient for the door scan, then fixates on the slit between the lift doors as they scream pass ground—the call button for that floor has been hacked out and taped over—it's just a flash of light that quickens her heart. Then the lift empties her into the safety of the fifty-third, the FarmTower control room, one of a dozen in the city heart. Tak's eyes are slits that appraise the slack bastards in their three-grand chairs: fake-cheese-poof eating, waist-expanded boredom jocks, skin lit gray under the green wall-to-wall plant screens.

The head bastard, Southern Boss, waddles across her view. "We have an intermittent valve malfunction," he begins, stubbing his finger on the on-screen pipe array.

"Why do you need me?" she asks, chucking her 'sack on an empty hot-desk, and trying not to sound as bolshy as she knows she is.

"Tried everything," says Southern Boss. "Every time we send someone up there, nothing's wrong. Replaced the faulting valve twice."

"So, it's not the valve," says Tak, scribbling the part's number on her hand, above the thenar eminence southern cross allegiance tattoo. She unthreads her tool holster, slings it about her hips. Southern Boss passes her an old-skool paper plan in a tight roll; the grid's too big for tablet screen, the MegaCorp too cheap for soft condensed matter sheets.

"Good luck," he says. His grin is from the same school as Boss's back in Dubai, faux humanness from a man who can't remember what it was like to be tribal. No one cares about her, really, in the bigger context of the FarmTower MegaCorp. They care about her skills, about what she can do for them and for what price. Everything else is secondary, which Tak knows would be painfully apparent the moment she fails to deliver.

They've never tried everything.

Tak takes the lift right to the top, then stairs and ladders into the roof space. Through a swipe-door and she finds the valve, in a manifold right on the outer roof. It stares out on the endless sparkling skyline. Its control stick glows green: no problem. So she starts chasing lines. Must be a wire cross, somewhere in the valve's control path.

Tak hunts the paths like an animal tracker, down shafts, up floors and around bends; hours through the endless FarmTower grid, all while the moon slinks a sickly slip above the skyline. Each floor is a shock of elemental color: lime green leaf forests, vermillion tomatoes, golden grain heads. She skirts the color. Tak is a gray-world girl, made for the conduits and cables that support the farm. The living stuff is too reverent, too elemental. She knows her place.

Each run ends at the control room, or back at the valve. Sometimes the fault is glowing on a control room screen, sometimes not. She resists the slack bastard invites to drinkies after work; resists the official end of her day. But she doesn't solve it, and a rage glows warm inside. This is all just a system. The problem is discoverable, understandable. Must be.

The control room is quiet, now. She checks her tab-phone; nearly midnight. Shift change. She spends another seven-twenty degrees of the clock and still, nothing. This job is blowing her average, pissing her off. The fault hasn't come in a while now. She storms up the tower one more time. That fucking valve. She peers at it through the swipe-door's glass panel, glowing green control stick. She is running out of options, out of energy, out of consciousness. She thinks of her flat, not far away, the softness of the bed and its pillows. Then she thinks of her reputation, of Southern Boss coming back tomorrow without a fix.

She sinks down behind the door, mind a whirl of fantasy sleep, red strobes and hardware malfunction.

She wakes again, sore ass from the concrete, sore back from the hard door. Two seconds tick as she remembers what she's doing. Then she hears it: a soft, sneaky footfall, just one. Tak presses her teeth, groove in groove, ready to scare any lazy ass maint guy coming up the ladder. She inches up, ready to vent valve-directed rage at the guy, because the valve could take whatever she had without returning satisfaction.

Later, Tak doesn't know why she glances out the swipe-door window at this point. Maybe to make sure the valve is watching the anticipated display of mind-to-mind violence, so it knows what it's facing in her, and maybe it can stop fucking her around now. Maybe to confirm she really is in Sydney, biggest, baddest New Kingdom city-state in this former great southern land. But what she sees is a shadow; someone out there on the valve deck.

Tak swipes her pass and throws the door on its hinges. Half a second of clear view is all she gets of mutherfucker, but that's enough time to work out quite a lot. Like, this guy doesn't work for the company. He's tall and lean, broad-shouldered and black-suited from toes to fingertips. Balaclava, too. He's not here to help. A jack line umbilicals from his tab-phone to the valve control stick, a cut-down rig, built to be concealed. *Intermittent fault.* Tak connects those dots in an instant. He's fucking with that valve, probably for a while now.

"Hey!" she yells, though it's not necessary. He's seen her as soon as the door sprung its latch, and he's already moving, a black back against a black-and-sparkling skyline. He vaults across the barrier wall, onto the round-deck runway. Vanishes in a second flat.

Tak sprints after him, rage in her heart-lines, growl in her airway. Fucker on her turf! One shot of him and she's in her animal brain, her territorial center framing the labels she puts on him. *Saboteur. Trespasser. Violator.* She scrambles over the wall and hauls ass along the no-railing walkway, chasing tiny white bips that flash with every pace of his running gait. His arms flail in a strange pattern and he slows; Tak knows she's caught him now; the runway's ending at the building edge, nowhere to go. She gropes in her pocket for her tab-phone. One capture is all she needs to send his ass to the slammer.

Then, he's gone. Tak blinks, retinas telling lies. Like, that the fucker just went over the edge, up here on the sixty-ninth. She skids to the edge. The next 'scraper is a half-field away, and below, a pedbridge links them, an old one, barricaded and unlit, sides concrete-cancer pocked, shedding lime dust as the fucker lopes along the top.

Getting the fuck away.

Tak doesn't think too much as she falls over the edge. The thoughts she does have she tries to turn feline: land on your feet, roll if you need to, but not over the edge! It's further than she thinks. The impact jars her knee, puts a pain-snarl on her lips. But she's on the level with him again, on her feet, and after him.

He reaches the 'scraper and she expects him to climb the maint ladder. It ends before the pedbridge, but he could reach it. But he doesn't. He goes up the wall like a spider. Tak gets it then: the funny arm movements. GrippyFingers. He was putting them on.

He's almost up and over the wall before she reaches the ladder. She's losing him now; losing it herself. She leaps for the ladder and catches her hands; hauls up her body in a lat-dorsi fiber-popping moves. Expects him to be gone when she gets to the roof, but he's just standing there, five meters away by an open stairwell door.

Tak stumbles to standing. She whips the tab-phone from her pocket and points it at him. She knows she's spent: muscles frayed, all the adrenaline she has cashed in. But it's all worth it now.

"Got you," she gasps. He's got goggles under the balaclava, but the cam shot has transtex to strip his black suit, enough for an ID. She's won; average preserved.

The balaclava mask shifts—a grin—and he points his tab-phone cam straight back at her. "Nice work," he says.

Tak hears approval in that male voice, approval from a saboteur. Too confident. Rage pumps her flagging heart. "You're not getting away," she reminds him, her breath finally coming back. "Your life just changed, fucker."

They shoot at the same time, twin bursts of tungsten-powered flashlight. When the afterimage is gone, so is he. But the tab-phone screen glows with the black outline of him, caught: full-frontal, center-shot and stupid. She clutches the tab-phone, pacing, punching the app to strip the photo back to skin. In a moment, she'll have him.

But she doesn't. She punches the app again, not believing what it shows. Because the image is a white-out. The fucker was wearing a lined suit. Tak curses. Even the places the suit didn't cover are cleanskin: not a single tat or implant on his head, hands or feet, and the goggles blocked retina scan too.

Tak retraces her steps, cold frustration replacing victory. She looks down at the ladder and the pedbridge, peppered in *condemned* notices. She can't go back that way. Dead ends, all.

Now fucking what?

Thumper counts this night as one of his less auspicious moments, the type that generates new rules. He toes open his pad window while two hands and his other toe hold him on the building's edge. He's immune to vertigo now, has been for a long time, but the drop to the sill and the vault inside draw a hiss tonight.

He whips off the GFs and sticks his hand in his armpit,

clamping down the wind-frozen underarm suit wall on his smarting fingertips. *New rule, no doing jobs when injured.*

He sentinels between the two windows getting re-leveled, checking the pad out. One chair, one Webz neck-hugger. Ball of fluff still under the door. Undisturbed.

This should bring settlement, but it doesn't. He flicks through his tab-phone to the shot of the woman from the FarmCorp. Her ID is an oversaturated square, her face an angry flush. He transtexes the image to get at her skin. He zooms into her tatts, each mark a telltale of her lineage, her allegiance. The southern cross on her hand, FarmCorp's logo on her bicep, a huge curling phoenix around her middle. An industrial trophy. She's impressed someone big.

Thumper lets his head smack against the wall. He doesn't know what he's feeling when he looks at her. It's a little like the feeling he gets when he does something new, things other people have told him are impossible. And a little like the thrill of going down to ground level; letting your feet touch that dangerous and unfamiliar street turf, just for a second before you vault for elevation safety.

A smile twists his mouth. Time to get serious.

So Thumper strips his lead-foil suit and falls into the sweat-stinky chair. He curls his left pinkie around the jack-out trigger and lets the neck-hugger hijack his neural inputs. A moment later, he's fizzed into the Webz, which the plebs all say is just like the real world, except for the brake glowing in his top-right vision. But Thumper is not a pleb. The Webz is for limited things, like shopping, holidays and finding information. He knows he can't find out the whys here; whys are for philosophy. He doesn't know why he's doing this, only what must be known. Like who is this woman who followed him across a crumbling pedbridge?

Tak's body wakes her with the belated notice of a rough two days. It takes all the hot water her pad allows to get her standing straight, all the caffeine her heart can handle to snare thoughts together. Her fingers smart as she digs her own GFs out from beneath the bed-end and stuffs them in her sack; she feels better having them. But all this fighting—for physical and conscious competence—

occurs in private, and by the time she hits the FarmCorp fifty-third, she's got her mantle back on.

She reports in to Southern Boss; there's no real problem with the system, she says, they've had a saboteur.

Southern Boss grunts in a satisfied way, like this news confirms the way he views the world: every fucker's out to cheat you. So even if this news isn't good for business, it'll do for internal validation, and he's a man who likes that. "So you're done? Security takes over?" he asks, daring her to misstep, even at the end.

"Absolutely not," she says. "Got a shot of him." She neglects the story of *how*. Tak's spent much time thinking about whether to disclose the how: would it show commitment? Make her unique, the preferred fault-finder? But on balance, she thinks Southern Boss will see her as dangerously unconventional, even reckless, which she certainly is. And she realizes Southern Boss is too deep inside his own gravity well to know recklessness can exist with balancing traits. To him, she's a one-track idea, and she wants that track to be *competent*, not *crazy*.

"I want to run through it with Security, answer their questions, stay for the debrief." Besides, she doesn't mention, she wants to check that he didn't do anything else. The roof holds lots of other gear. But the possibility things went further might put Southern Boss in a dangerously over-reactive state, which would only make things inefficient.

Southern Boss leaves her to it, earning her the furtive eyes of all the control room jocks. She avoids them and makes for mid-floors.

A woman behind the Sec-desk plays with her tab-phone. Tak glimpses cats; one of those vids where they make mistaken leaps and crash into walls. The woman looks cross when Tak clears her throat.

"Yes?"

"Have an image for a new case file. Southern Boss just called it down."

The woman doesn't believe her; or at least, punishes her for interrupting the cats. Tak has her badge scrutinized, is made to wait. When she finally sees the Sec-head, her heart is seething. Sec-head takes a copy of the shot.

"Can't do much with this," he says, sucking his teeth, which seem unnaturally white to Tak; probably just paid a bomb for new-falsies. "He's a cleanskin. Useless in the databases. Cops'll tell us the same thing."

"He's not a cleanskin," she protests. "He's just wearing a lined suit."

Sec-head shrugs. *Same diff.*

Tak almost says, *what about a biomet database,* one that matches his build, the breadth of his ankle bones, the nuances in his biometrics, but she stops herself. That stuff's only for the Kingdom cops. Otherwise, its Webz territory, not exactly legal. And there's no way she's going there. She's better than this guy; there'll be a way.

This enthusiasm lasts the fives minutes it takes for the lift to deliver her back to the fifty-third. She sinks into her hot-desk, trolls the old 'Net for half a clock-turn, turning up nothing but ill-maintained personal pages and rubbish from forty years ago. After all, what can she search for? Black-suited saboteur in Sydney-state?

Later, she's infiltrated with the sense of being watched. The other jocks are floating around her desk. One particularly nervous one tries a smile. "We're going for a drink?" he says, cutting his sentence into a weird half-way house of statement and question, in case she throws the idea back like an incendiary device.

But Tak's all out of the stuff inside her that makes ammunition. She's aware of her status having slipped. Her problem has loose ends, she's come down a level. And that makes her more accessible to these guys. Later, she knows this will make her angry again, but right now she does want a drink, and has no idea where to find one.

The New Ship Inn is two 'scrapers over, several levels above what Tak assumes was the old inn, and perched on the once-Circular Quay, now overdomed to connect the tunnel portals to the hydrocraft terminal, and stuffed with city cops to keep the terminal to ground floor interface clean. The Inn itself is retro-styled: one long bar with gleaming chrome taps, gaming stations, pay-per-use Webz terminals corralled behind a partition in the back, and round tables crowded with a melancholic after-shift crowd. Speakers spill vintage dark rock that reflects off the discrete plexibarrier separating the bar from the clientele. Drinks are ordered from touch terminals in the table centers; very retro.

The control room jocks are universally awful companions. Tak has five minutes' patience for their talk, which is full of FarmCorp in-references and movies she hasn't seen. One guy is particularly persistent, especially after he's shot a few glasses and filled the other jocks with laugh-worthy jokes. Tak recognizes his type: king of the small social mountain, growing his entitlement with each ethanol molecule escaping his liver. She slips away to a corner table, where she faces the speaker point blank. The bass massages her headache. Maybe she should take one of those Webz terminals, lock in and find a Sven, or better, a dojo where she can smack someone in the face, and it feel mostly real.

"Self-medicating?"

A shadow slips into an empty chair beside her, facing the bar while she faces the pulsing wall. Tak goes to tell the jock to fuck off, but one glance tells her this isn't him. This is foil-reflective aviators on a young man's face. High forehead, real hair in a natural dark shade. Plain black shirt and pants. Tall and lean. Seen him before. She feels for her tab-phone through her pants.

"Leave it there," he says. "Just be a waste of effort."

"That's what you think." She glares at him, irises ringing poison. He's given her a bad day, and two bad nights, and now he's being cocky. She bets those glasses are lead-lined too. "I didn't ID you," she says, in case he's a dangerous type, like this might dissuade him from whatever fiendish plan he has behind that smooth face.

"I know," he says. "But I got you." He smiles. It's a nice one.

"Big deal," she says, but it is. If he has her ID, he knows where she works, where she lives, how much she earns and where she stashes it. Enough to follow her here. And she has nothing on him. She needs to know if she's in danger of harm, or just in danger of irritation. So she says, "What do you want?"

"Buy you a drink?"

Tak looks down at her still half-full glass of nameless buzz diluting in melted ice, and thinks about date rape. "No."

"Thought as much."

She wants to hate him, or be afraid of him, anything that will make him different and wrong. But he's also a problem, which is intriguing. The music two-steps with her anger, but the image of him as an anonymous, black-clad saboteur is slipping. He seems too safe. She can't maintain both views of him at once.

"So, back to the start. Self-medicating?" he asks.

"Obviously not," she says, pushing the glass away. The speaker is silent a beat before the next track erupts, more up-tempo.

"I don't mean the drink. I mean the music," he says, tipping his head back towards the speaker. "You had a bad day. They all"—he traces a finger through the air, capturing the bar's crowd—"had a bad day. So, you go for musical medication. Angry music for angry emotions. That's why you don't like the drink. It deadens what you're feeling and, really, you want to feel it. More of it. The track gives you that. And when you feel validated, you can sleep."

Tak stares at him. Irritation flares like lit accelerant. But it's as much towards the pulsing speaker as him. She wants to get away from the noise now, to test his theory, or avoid testing it. Wants to get into one of those Webz terminals.

"Do you always spout such crap?" she asks. But she knows he's seen her eyes working. He knows she thought about it.

"I have a few theories," he says.

"Save it," she growls. Because she sees him again on that FarmCorp rooftop, fucking with her valve. How easily he could have gotten away, but he'd taunted her. She can't just leave. "You're just as bad," she shoots at him.

He raises his eyebrows above the aviators. "Oh I am?"

She struggles over the music. "I'm guessing you fuck up other people's stuff for a living, but you're not content with that. No, you have to pose. Something deep inside you recognizes your occupation is useless and valueless, so you need someone to validate you, even a nobody like me."

His smile is genuine now. Tak gets the urge to slug him, bypass the whole going-to-the-Webz shit and just get it done right here. *And then get sprung by the cops for battery.* With great effort, she pulls the tab-phone from her pocket and pointedly strides for the door.

Thumper knows what he's doing right now is pretty stupid, even when he's protected from ID. Or thinks he's protected. But he doesn't care. He's interested. She's leaning on the wall outside the bar now, waiting for the lift.

"You're wrong about that," he tells her.

"What?" she snaps.

"The last thing you said. But it was interesting. I think it says more about you, Takeshi."

Her mouth tightens, her arms bunch like she wants to hit him. He expects her anger; she's scared of him now, a little, and maybe he's even made her job hard. The lift opens, empty and bright.

"Don't you use my name. I don't know yours," she grinds at him.

"Thumper," he offers.

"That's not a real name," she says.

"Real enough." Then, before she can leave, he says, "Come out tomorrow night?" He wants to pursue this conversation. It's been a long time since Thumper spoke to anyone who could keep him interested.

But she gives him a look that defines loathing, one that says how stupid is it for him to ask? She's leaving his sorry ass where it belongs. And soon, she's inside the lift.

"You should be afraid of me," she says, as the doors close. And Thumper has to wonder then if she isn't right.

Three hours pass and Thumper's already late, which he's done on purpose. He slinks through the back Webz, a mean part of the non-endorsed sectors, feigning alarm as best he can. The people he works for appreciate scruples more than punctuality, and he needs to play them that way, which is either incredibly brave or incredibly stupid, and probably both.

To get inside the gentleman's club, he steps over discarded programming junk, broken parts of shoes and fried chicken dinners. In the endorsed parts of the Webz, cleaner worms eat this kind of thing for fat government fees. But no one in the non-endorsed servers pays for that shit. So, as Thumper boots the pile aside, he executes a little code that protects his digital self from contamination; you never know what other programmers might shove in rotting detritus. He'd heard that once, in the endorsed Webz, a parasitic worm in a junk pile had hijacked a cleaner-worm and overwritten its subroutines with something elegant and destructive. Then the parasitized super-worm had escaped its bounds and eaten out two blocks of endorsed Webz shopping mall before they'd even found a coder with the balls to take it on. Thumper thinks about this. He detects elements of untruth in his memory of just 'hearing' about this story. Clearly, he still has some mental work to do before his recollections are changed enough to convince others, such as the men he works for.

The gentleman's club, a den of old-school wood and green felt with sodium-yellow shaded lights, is populated with a mix of straight and twisted types from all over the real world, drawn to 1890s frontier amusements in the form of corseted wenches and the tinkling of a saloon piano. Thumper slides around the lounge floor, aiming for the telecoms terminal he knows is in the hall, and playing with his stubble, which never feels quite right in the Webz.

A man in a flight suit stands by a hideously rendered and anachronous floor-to-ceiling fish tank, studded with exotic coral and fish with trailing fins. Thumper perceives the ripple of interference; blocking any eavesdropping. For this is José.

"Why is this here?" says José "Did they have fish in the old west?"

Thumper puts his hand to the telecoms terminal, as if José is someone he's just accidentally met here. "Written by a junk coder," he says, shrugging. "Maybe the owner's kid, who knows. Sentiment endorses all kinds of bad taste."

José laughs. His teeth flash like a dental restoration ad. His blond, sculpted hair is from the catalogue entry *Pitt, Brad circa 1996*. Thumper tries not to notice these things, but it's like trying not to notice how the fish-tank coder used a time-expensive routine to render any curves, so they pixelate whenever a fish passes by. José's like that too; every time they meet, he distorts Thumper's reality for a while, when Thumper wonders if the global powers so much bigger than him—aka José's terrapilot bosses—are really playing him at levels where his consciousness can't even go.

"Speaking of bad taste ..." says José. He hands across something that looks like a rolled-up magazine, a pair of breasts bulging from the glossy outer curve. Thumper knows what it is: a private protocol written to resemble a titty-mag. He takes it, and from then on, hears José's voice only in his head.

What do you need? José says.

Thumper says, *This isn't secure, you know.*

It's as secure as things get here. Need to be as good as you to break this thing.

Thumper grunts. There aren't many like him. *I need a tracking trace.*

José groans. *Let me guess. That agri fault-finder you asked me about last time?*

Thumper's silence answers that one.

What are you doing, T?

Thumper lays it out quick. *Might have put her in some harm. She's trying to ID me and she's going to keep at it. But my job's still open and these guys don't play nice. I just want to keep an eye on her.*

José winces; terrapilots are straight as arrows, and Thumper knows this talk of a 'job' will punch José's conflicted buttons. *I don't want to know. You know you can do better than this.*

There's a moment like this in every one of their conversations, where José becomes the fatherly voice of concern. Thumper always wonders if the guy isn't a sixty-something ex-marine in a neck-hugger in some government office, on a covert convert mission targeting the stray-but-talented coders of the world.

He pushes. *Just need to know if she enters the Webz. Don't need anything real world.*

José thinks a beat, then pulls the magazine back and stuffs it in one Tardis-like pocket. "Just a minute." He disappears into a door marked *Men's*. Five minutes later, when he's made a good show of watching the pixelated angelfish, Thumper pushes through the same door. Inside, the coders haven't bothered with render at all. The room is a white box, with four curtained spaces. Three are open, a simple bar-style stool inside, where a long-jacked Webz user can use their sophisticated jack-in system for relief, or where such sophistication is not in their budget, jack-out with a tagged return point to use the real-world facilities. Thumper throws open the fourth curtain. On the stool is a thumb-sized token of soft condensed matter, its substance dim but for a slowly blinking red circle.

Thumper seizes the tracker and makes for the exit. Time to see the men who hired him for the FarmCorp job. He sequences his arguments, practicing as he goes, correcting the words until he believes them as truth. *No, I can't execute the next phase, not yet. They found the first fault, so care is needed.* No, this is not confident. *They found the first fault as expected.* No, they don't need to know that. That will make them nervous. *All is in order. Two more days. Wait for the fault-finder to be gone; then the target is easy. Just as planned.*

Thumper keeps on with this, refining, buffing, but in deep truth he knows. He could do the job tonight; he could finish it. So why is he pushing out the timetable? The argument to have Tak gone is a good one, it will work on the men who hired him, because it sounds logical. But Thumper knows she won't leave. Not with that look in her eye; that fire that wants him beaten. He feels like the first time he played chess against someone good, someone good enough to challenge him. Waiting for the next move.

The rest of Tak's night is not a good one. She storms back to Security to point her finger, point it hard. She's been *followed*, she tells them, shaking the pic of Thumper in his giddy, fuck-you black. Their alarm is initial relief, until she finds out what it means. Here, the desk girl says, fill this out. She passes over a tab-form. Tak takes in two things: that the form is a hundred tab screens, and that once she fills it, she'll be in lock-down. No more on-the-job, not until this was resolved. Tak sees her career evaporate into administrative wait-space. She leaves so fast the Sec girl spins in her chair.

Back in her tiny, one-window living box, she racks another few hours trolling the networks for legal access to biometrics. Nada. This stuff is off-limits, the realm of Kingdom agency privacy laws, which means she has to interest the cops. Tak pauses, hands over keyboard keys like a raptor's kill strike on pause. She could go to the cops direct, but that bypasses Security, a breach of FarmCorp protocol. She imagines the glittery fire-your-ass hard-on in Southern Boss's eyes at that one.

Midnight passes like a missed highway sign, then the threshold for sleeping too. Tak rubs her eyes, imagines facing Southern Boss in the morning. Imagines other options.

Before dawn can erupt, she's shot down twenty floors to the building's level five pedbridge, a pulsating link stuffed with all-night caffeine purveyors and illicit, lingering tobacco. Near the end is a HarpoonWebz, a chain-joint Webz host, sporting rows of privacy-curtained, lockable Webz access chairs, each embroidered with their logo—a smiling white whale stuck with a neck-hugger shaped 'poon—glowing blue-purple and brilliant white under black lights and neon. Tak swipes her tab-phone at a booth, locks in and locks on, and a moment later she's jacked into Webz central Syd. Harpoon's patented jack-in portal looks like a vintage *Star Trek* transporter deck, and Tak stalks off the podium, giddy as her brain accepts Harpoon's algorithms, and into the giant, simulated Sydney night.

It takes less time than she expects to find the seedy edges of endorsed Webz space. Beyond what the Kingdom pays to render, the blanks fill with unvetted providers. Some are legit shopfronts, others are squatter-types: domain-hackers with a front for illegal goings-on-in-the-back routines. Tak knows the Sprinks shut down these spring-ups with regularity, but high-profits mean they sprout again and again, the hydras of quantum bandwidth.

Tak sees one now, a quick-rendered nail salon, meshed in a mostly-blank side-alley. The store almost looks right, but the services bulletin says, *gel tips, instant authentic!, profiling, best for love!,* and she knows enough to read between. They hack bioprofiling data for people who want to hook up with the cute commuter they just snapshotted across the transporter. A promo-girl in a Manga costume nods her pigtails in Tak's direction, offering a flyer.

"Nails?" she asks, flashing a ten-set of gleaming, blue hypersparkle. "Best for love?" She winks.

And for a hair-thin moment, Tak is going in there. She's giving them the shot of Thumper, and she's finding out who he is. Then, her eyeballs rest on that southern cross on her hand. She thinks about what it means to have allegiance to an idea. She believes in the New Kingdom, believes in her work and the company behind it, feeding the world. Will she really lose her morals just to maintain her average?

Fuck.

She stalks back to a caffeine vendor and takes a double hit of crema. She scowls down the alley as she sips, caught in a vortex. She wants him bad, wants that smug, black-clad, no-tatted ass to go down for what he's done.

What he's done. *What is that*, whispers a voice, *screwed with a valve stem*? Managed to piss you off? He's just joining the queue. Tak glares into the artificially prolonged crema bubbles. She glances back at the salon.

By now, Thumper should be jacked out and paying the sandman, but instead, he's pumping through the skyline. He stretches in a leap, GFs sticking the counter-gs around a banner pole. He lands atop the pedbridge and checks his watch; ten minutes since the tracker started glowing green. Not bad. He pulls a secret agent pancake to peer in a window, sees the usual assortment of coffee-pushers and cybersmoking dens oozing tantalizing scents. His heart slams against his chest in rhythm of a hunt. He slips into a balcony, feeling the tracker's heading like a migrating-bird-brain in his center forehead. Not far. Not far.

He spies the faux-nail salon with a skip of nausea. The guys who hire him probably run it. He itches, somewhere low in his skull; he wonders if he'll have to go inside, thinks about how he could hide himself if he does. The brake glows in his top-right vision. He could dump the brake. But risky, being marooned that way.

Was she worth it?

He slips down the alley, but the tracker's heading swings around. She's not down there at all. He sees her wedged in a caffeine pusher's corner couch, a light streak of skin against the black velvet booth. The next instant he's slipped inside the booth, thinking: the coder who wrote this velvet wasn't that good; it's too smooth, nearly polished on the fingertips, tripping the senses with visual disagreement.

Then he remembers why he's here.

Tak seems defeated. "Don't worry, I didn't go in there," she says. Thumper feels relief like a rain shower, and tries not to show it.

"You wouldn't have gotten anything for it anyway," he tells her. "I'm not in biometrics."

She snorts. "Of course you are. If you weren't you wouldn't be able to travel. And I'm sure saboteurs travel an awful lot."

He gives her a quick smile, one that he knows looks good on his avatar with its skull-trimmed hair. "There's ways to alter data."

"Then you'd never be able to cross a border."

"You make it sound like the only way across a border is through security."

She is shocked at this; he sees it plainly. She doesn't like him. Doesn't like that he doesn't value the rules she does. And he doesn't want it to be like that. "We're not so very different," he tries, hoping she'll argue with him, keep this interesting.

Her look hardens like overcooked toffee. "You must be deluded." She starts to edge around the booth and escape him.

"You don't do your job for the money and neither do I," he says. "There's one thing common."

She comes back at him with a pointed finger. "You don't have a *job*," she accuses. Thumper admires the render of her hair as she moves. "You stop other people from doing *theirs*. You make work for other people."

Thumper laughs. "The world's bigger than you think," he says. "You suppose, then, that some jobs are more useful than others?"

She edges away again, so he keeps talking. "Like, for example, a doctor is more useful than sewer maint guy?" He stares at her. She hesitates; simultaneously thinking and trying to find a way out.

"Yeees," she concedes.

"Why?"

Her eyes slide sideways, trying to rationalize. "Because a doctor saves lives. And the sewer guy just maintains a system."

"But would you also acknowledge that the city goes to shit if the sewers don't work? And that makes the doc's work harder? Makes work for them?"

She purses her lips. "Yes."

Thumper nods. "It's bigger than that. The doc can only do their work if there are designers and fabricators to make the tools. If there are teachers to educate them. We're all co-dependent.

Everything needs everything else to work properly. The sewer guy is as useful as the doc."

"That's different! Neither of them are destroying other people's systems!"

Thumper feels the smile creases drop from his skin. "It doesn't matter. How do you know what the people who hire me want?" he says. "The whole world's food production is corporatized and mechanized. Do you really know what they're doing? What if the guys that hired me are looking for evidence? Collusion, maybe. Poisoning."

Tak's avatar shifts. "Are they?"

"I don't ask. My point is, I'm just as useful as you. The system has room for what I do."

She gives him a disgusted look, but with less heart. Then, as she's edging away again, he adds, "Do you realize you're in danger?"

That stops her. Thumper leans in. "I advise you against trying to pin me. I have no idea what the guys behind this might do. Try if you want to, but don't ever come into the Webz to the illegits. I'm not in there anyway, and you'll just flag yourself as someone who knows too much. And if you *are* going to try it, at least be smart! Don't jack in with a registered provider like you are right now, and definitely not so close to home. Got it?"

Thumper tries to say this without passion, but he doesn't like the idea she'll be reckless on his account.

She rolls her eyes. "So convinced, aren't you, that I'd come down to your level. I don't need illegits. I'm better than that. And I'm going to get you anyway."

She unjacks right in front of him. Thumper blinks once as the Webz render refreshes the space Tak had occupied in a flurry of mismatched pixels. She mustn't be far from the jack-in point, but he knows she'll still have a ripping headache. Hurt herself, just to escape him. He doesn't like it.

Tak spends the night dancing with an unfamiliar feeling. When she was very small, her father had taken her on a sailboat across a lake, which had seemed like crossing the ocean. Tak had been scared of the deep water, knowing that even muddy farm puddles could hide greebs and stones. And then, the storm had come. The sails had snapped like whips, and the steel-gray, lightning-streaked front had boiled across the lake.

Now, overdosed on codeine from the post-remote-jack-out headsplit, she has that feeling again. A storm gathering in the rear-vision. Thumper's words have burrowed into her psyche, exposing the weak wood. Because she's seen things in her years as a fault-finder. She's wondered about how the FarmCorp runs. But those things have always been filed under zero-care-factor.

She finds Southern Boss waiting for her in the control room.

"It's closed," he announces, sitting her down. "Security's done with it. They're fencing the roof pad, putting a camera up there too. You're done."

Tak feels panicked; threads of incompleteness slipping her fingers. "But the guy—"

"Doesn't matter," says Southern Boss, linking his fingers across his risen-bun-dough of a gut. "Minor league perp. Didn't do much damage. You did good." He smiles that predatory smile. His eyes say, I'm done with this, don't push it.

"But I'm not finished," says Tak.

"Of course not," says Southern Boss. "There's the report to do. Hot-desk is yours until tomorrow. I'll have the Scram for you then. System malfunction in an irrigator up in Arizona, if you'll take it?"

Here is that moment again. The one where his binary view of her can be set to *useful/sane* or *difficult/crazy*. She swallows her disquiet. "Sure," she says.

So she writes up the report in a daze. There's not much to write; even by FarmCorp standards. She treks to the roof for good measure, checking the system numbers she's given. By knock-off, the report is complete and thorough. She leaves it unsubmitted, in case she remembers anything more, and leaves to sleep on it.

But somehow, an hour later, the elevator doors are opening on the New Ship Inn. She wonders if this is a good idea, but if she's right, she's *right*, and tomorrow she's on a Scram anyway. She slips past the bar, each table thick with patrons like zombies on a kill. In the screened back room, she eyes the dingy Webz terminals. These are bring-your-own-lock. A lock purchasing machine is hung with an out-of-order sign. She pretends to search for the least soiled seat, but really she's looking at the registration units. She bets there are none. This is that kind of place.

So she's not surprised when she spies Thumper, leaning against the very back wall, black-suited like the first time, glasses in place, every bit his avatar. She's been so fixated on him, he seems like an old friend. She struggles to remember to hate him.

"This is much better," he says, indicating the illegally unregistered Webz jacks.

"If you have enough money for the fine," she shoots back.

He gives her a quick smile. "Have to catch you first. The Sprinks aren't that good with climbing towers."

"Spoken from experience."

He shakes his head. "Spoken from logic and observation of their tactics. I don't work in the Webz."

Tak finds this interesting; she leans on the wall beside him. "Worried about black ICE?"

He glances down at her sidelong, appraising her. "What do you know about black ICE?"

She shrugs. "Digital security that kills the intruder. All the MegaCorps have it. You've seen the rallies, right?" From time to time, the news feeds show black ICE protests, placards that called it digital murder.

Thumper nods, the edges of his eyes creasing. "Sure, I've seen them. But no. Black ICE is a ridiculous fantasy."

"What?"

"The MegaCorps want you to believe they can do it, but it's bullshit. You can't kill someone with a neural jack-in. Best you can do is seize them, maybe, but at some level, consciousness drops out and the neurotransmitters are exhausted. Blue ICE is far more dangerous."

"What the fuck's blue ICE?"

Thumper grins. "Getting ID'ed by a security system. That's why I don't work in the Webz. Blue ICE takes your ID, then drops your brake. Leaves you adrift in the Webz without ability to jack-out. Sprinks bust you. Laws are murky. Never work again, either 'cause they mark you, or they end you."

Tak shudders. The world has become too large. Her shoulder is against Thumper's now. "The job's over," she says softly. "They closed it today. I'm on a Scram tomorrow."

He looks at her again, and this time, she holds his eyes. "Can I show you something?" he says.

"Does it involve clambering over buildings? Because I left my GrippyFingers at home."

"Trust me?" he asks. And she lets him take her hand.

His place is in a dodgy quarter, across the harbor in a high-rise stuck with dozens of linking pedbridges.

"What, you don't use the door?" she asks, lunging her boot through his window and hoping not to crack her head on the frame.

"Not if I can help it," he says, easing in after her, far more gracefully. He takes stock of the place before moving on. It's bare except for a bed and a chair with a Webz neck-hugger, which looks expensive. Thumper latches a plexibarrier over the window and closes the blind.

"What is this you're going to show me?" she asks.

"Have a seat." She sits on the bed edge and he stands before her, takes off his jacket. When he catches the hem of the shirt, he pauses. "Don't freak out," he says.

He pulls it off, and Tak stares. He's well-built; long muscles built for urban chase. But he is completely unmarked.

"Why don't you have any tatts?" she demands. She's never seen anyone without them. Cleanskins are allegianceless spies, parts played in movies by actors who have to cover up their own marks. She springs up and circles him, scrutinizing the skin for make-up or signs of old ones removed. When she sees nothing, she touches him gently, in the center of his chest to check if he is real.

"I never got any," he says, brushing his fingers over hers. "I grew up a long way from here and I avoided all the markings. It's a long story."

"What about here?" she asks him, pointing at his pants.

He loses those too, and his shoes, until he's naked for her scrutiny. And still, not a mark. Tak remembers who he is, the trouble he's caused. But then she's standing in front of him, her hands on his body, knowing he's looking back at her. Knowing he wants her.

"You must make a lot of money," she says softly, as his lips seek hers, her hair a tangle in his fingers. She wants him to say something that gets her distance back, something that she can resent about him.

"Look around you," he says against her cheek. "Money's for what you need. And it amplifies any insecurities. A jerk is a bigger jerk when they're loaded, you ever notice that?"

Tak feels the delicious slide of his lips on her cheek. But she thinks of Southern Boss, of all the bosses, and their narrow-minded, money-honed focus. "Yeah," she says. "I noticed." She is going to ask him more, but he kisses her then, and the question is lost.

When Thumper wakes in the morning, Tak is already gone. He sits a long time, thinking on his next move, avoiding smoothing the sheets crumpled where she lay. Not ready to erase her like that. Not yet.

Tak has her travel 'sack with her in the control room the next morning. She's been here for an hour now, an hour before Southern Boss is due in. Her hand hovers over *submit*, a tangle of conflict dancing in her synapses and preventing the final stroke.

Some things have not added together. Thumper is smart, she knows that. He's also incredibly valuable to someone. So this job just seems too trifling. Just a saboteur screwing with a low importance valve. The report is barely twenty pages; nothing in FarmCorp. Insignificant. Which means: will be overlooked.

Tak pulls her hand back from the panel. She gets a bad feeling. She checked the roof already, but she's missing something. She pulls up plans, looking at what's *inside* the roof's swipe-door. Switchboards. HVAC system fans. Then, Tak swears. Off the hall, is a tiny lettered note on the plans: *RDT. Remote diagnostic terminal.* It's a link-point into the main system, meant for routine maintenance. And she suddenly gets it. Every time he screwed with the valve, FarmCorp sent someone up there, who opened the door. Which would have let Thumper in and to that terminal. So, he mucked with the valve as many times as he needed to access the system. Dripping something in.

Tak curses, feeling played, feeling stupid. Feeling when she shouldn't have been. She scrambles for her tab-phone, even as the sinking dread scrambles her responses. She has no idea what he's planted, but she knows they're about to have a very serious malfunction.

Thumper's not even really out of bed before it happens. He hears the bootfall in the hallway, an unfamiliar tread that is not his neighbor or a delivery guy. He bothers only with his pants, and digs for the GrippyFingers at the bed-end. He can hear creaking outside, too: weight on the fire escape.

And his GrippyFingers aren't there. He gives himself three seconds to rip up the mattress and pat around on the floor, but nothing. Panic gets its talons in. And he remembers: Tak being here last night, her laughing that he kept his GFs in the same place she did. Oh, Jesus Christ.

A knock comes on the door. And no one ever knocks on his door. He thinks about going for the window, but he can imagine what else she's told them. *He goes in through the window. He's good at climbing. Exits here, here, and here.*

Fuck, he's been stupid.

He throws himself into the bathroom and locks the door. A panel above the toilet leads to a pipe shaft. Thumper replaced the screws with double-sided, quarter-turn fasteners the first day he got here, so the panel's off in two seconds, and he pulls it closed behind him. Buys a few minutes.

He climbs using the bolted pipe joints, his naked fingers slipping on the slick, dusty steel. He counts access panels as he goes; there's a pedbridge at three and six levels up, but only the six-up access panel is in a communal bathroom. He hopes he won't fall before he gets there.

He can't hear anything below, can't hear anything except his ragged breath, and the thoughts panic helpfully brings. Things like, *you're fucked buddy.* Then, the mental equivalent of a slow-hand clap. Well, fuck that.

He reaches six levels, the access panel a square of light in the dark wall. He doesn't want to do this twice, so he hangs on his hands, abs screaming, and kicks with both feet. The crummy bathroom plasterboard ruptures like a clown's cream pie, and next moment he's through into the tiled space, shedding white dust like an old-time steam-train.

Around the corner is the pedbridge, and freedom. He can replace the GFs, replace the Webz hugger. Easy.

But around the corner is a bunch of cops, and a barricade. And Thumper suddenly realizes: this is how it is all over the building. Every pedbridge. She told them well.

It's at that moment he knows what he should have done. He should have gone to ground, down to the street level where the city is meaner than the cops, where Thumper'd be as likely to get killed as get away, at least a fifty-fifty chance.

And he's thinking that still when they cuff him and cart him away.

They take him to the cophouse, another multistory with bright, white cells and bright, white teeth in the interviewer's mouth.

"Name?" says the cop, pen paused above his tab-form. He's got a young head of hair and an old-worn look of a man who only works for the money.

Thumper just grins at him.

"Like that, is it?" says the guy. "Fine."

So, the cop scans his biometrics and punches the scanner card into the terminal. Five seconds later, he frowns, just as Thumper's expecting. "Identity cloaking is a very serious offense," says the cop.

Thumper knows where it goes from here, and his mind is blazing. If he was in the Webz, he'd be better equipped. Escape is pure software. But the hard reality of bricks and mortar is different. He's got to draw deeper in his history. He turns to the watching camera in the corner. "I would like to speak to my lawyer," he says carefully.

The cop rises wearily, and pushes across the desk-mounted tab-phone. Thumper tries not to get too excited. He has to be clear to code this one. But he knows; he can see it all. The tab-phone runs on the central system, so he has a way in. The cameras run on it too. He can jam them all. And the sprinklers—now there's an idea—their deluge valves are system-controlled too. He learnt about that when planning the FarmCorp job. So to buy time, to cover the fact he's opened a command line on the tab-phone, he calls the only person he knows with an untraceable, iron-clad security wall: José.

"Hey," he says, as the call goes through. *Hey, the greeting that means I'm in trouble.*

"Hey," returns José. "That agri fault-finder get you after all?"

"I'm in a coptower," he says.

"You're not seriously asking—"

"No, nothing like that. Just needing a little time," he says. *Keep talking, don't you get it?*

A pause. A sigh. "Was she worth it?"

The question punches through Thumper's concentration like a ballistic round. If Tak's found the job he set at FarmCorp, she's in some serious trouble. "Need your help with that, too," Thumper says. Then he makes it happen. Execute. Lights go out. Execute. A rush of water. His fingers slip.

"What the fuck's that noise?" says José.

"Gotta go," says Thumper, grabbing the bioscan card.

Tak hears about it in the Scram terminal, just before she escapes to the Arizona corn belt. She watches the wet cops fending off desperate, hungry journos and freelance clip-posters. She sees the embarrassment in their tight-drawn mouths. Suspect escaped. A smile lifts her lips, even as she's shitted they lost him. She's won in the end; found the sabotage before it took them down, stayed employed. But her smile is mixed. It's part admiration. Part intrigue. Part wanting to know if she could do it again.

So, she wonders what's waiting in Arizona. Knowing he's still in the world.

THE MESSAGE

He had once been more than just *brother*.

Siah had been son, cousin. Even *father*. Then had ruined each and all, kinships become ghosts, other selves.

But *brother* … he'd counted on that to his end. Now he wondered if it counted at all.

His remaining sister held the precious paper for him to take, its edges already wrinkled, its tip shaking in her grasp. Even on his knees to remind him of her station, his lip wanted to curl; he hesitated just to slight her. Seer or no, this message was a mistake, one she made for them all. But she stared him down, that knowing look, the one that said she knew his will to disobey her.

"Go, brother."

Her command was law. Even when it sent him into the wastes at night, where he could become Drel-hunted, or fall in a sewer crevasse, or be killed by the enemy watch. So he left her in a puddle of murmuring voices and made a show of leaving, dutiful *brother*, messenger into the dangerous night.

As he went down the feet-tracked hall, his vision fuzzied as it did whenever he left her. The carpet, worn to its under-threads, smudged whole again. Walls, peeling and bloomed with mildew, blurred uniform gray. Multiverse-many, he saw them all, and all but one was probabilistic uncertainty. Quantum vision, a cursed thing. And he knew he could betray himself at any moment; when his gaze flickered just so, his propensity for fuck-ups. He coughed; let his eyelids droop.

The other hunters huddled in the battery room, by the stacked acid barrels with their tangled wire coat. The grubby maps in their fists were a gray mass, and a scavenged bulb shed a turbulent glow. Siah kept his gaze down, squint in place as they gathered round. *No point getting killed now.* But their relief was his irritation. None would go with him, none would offer, such were these men. Hunters, not brothers.

"Thank gods it's over."

"Will you take the ninety-six?"

"Watch saw deer in the hollow, might be Drels there too."

"None of the motors are running." This one was an apology.

Siah let them talk while they proffered arms. He strapped a knife at his thigh, and another blade in the hollow of his back; stuffed a revolver in his belt. Two rounds; better than nothing.

Then he stretched down—somewhat to test his strapping, but mostly to hide his eyes. They hurt as he controlled the flicker; it was strong, an unleashed animal after being tempered by his sister so long.

More reason to get gone.

He feigned a pensive look, out the window. Formed a plan, but kept it loose and changeable. Down the ninety-six to the message circle, or maybe through the side tracks. If no one's there, through to the mall ground. Or not. Across the wastes to their Hold. Or maybe that will never be. And all he said to them was, *Don't expect me till morning.*

The Hold inhabitants watched, anxious in the upper windows, as he strode out the heavy doors, double thick and barred, and through the palisade of stakes and sharpened steel. But they closed the doors behind him, and then he was alone.

Down the hill and over the wall, he crept inside the ruin-infested forest. The moon waned, half-destroyed, like the city that had stood here before the Event: a violation that had smudged out nearly all existence. The lunar glow made skeletons of the new trunks and rimmed craters in the failing rooftops. But all of this was blurred for him, savage beauty softened. Siah hated that he saw this uncertainty, the true nature of the universe; that the world doubted its own future. Siah certainly doubted his. No one else within the Hold saw these things. With his sister's cancelling presence, he could pretend normalcy. Without her ... he was vulnerable. And now he was alone.

So why had she sent him?

He fingered the message, a lump in his belt leather, wondering if the whole point was to put him in harm's way. He was a liability, she risked herself protecting him; but had it come to that? Siah growled, frustrated. His brand of quantum alteration was not hers: he was blind. She was a Seer; ergo, she saw. She was useful. He was a filthy Q-liner, a thing both label and consequence, spoken of only when the fires burned low and the Hold's men were drunk and brave. *Impulsive quantum universe fuckers.* Bad luck bringers. *Kill on sight.* And no one knew but her.

Her voice returned to him in a whisper. *Go, brother ...*

Siah slunk from the forest to the old ninety-six, a grassy corridor littered with rusted car husks. He wove between cover, trying not to think of his destination: the message circle, a bare asphalt ring under a dead thrusting trunk that had enveloped a buckled highway sign in its growth. Rumor said that the circle was where a Q-liner had lost it; that they'd unwritten the fabric of the universe here and reassembled it. Cursed ground. That was why nothing would grow. Siah didn't believe it; if a Q-liner had really done it, the patch would have been the size of the city.

He stopped short of the circle, his fist working the message until the flimsy folds softened. He hadn't expected anyone to be here, and they weren't. Not after the last time.

Then, the enemy had organized an exchange. They'd send a junior hunter, one who didn't get it. That you didn't *plan* in this world. Concrete intent got you killed or taken. Drels lurked in the forest wastes, they saw probable opportunity. Siah played with the paper, unfolding and refolding it, one-handed. He re-lived that day. Ten crisp seconds of certainty chute, when his vision had cleared because the outcome was sure.

That simple news relay became ambush. Drels had killed four and taken three in breathless speed. At the time, Siah had been sure he had not done anything to promote it. He hadn't lost time; hadn't made a quantum switch. No reversis, no ripples. Nothing to indicate he'd slipped. But afterwards, doubt had come. He'd stuck closer to his sister, where the multiverse couldn't tempt him, where the hunters couldn't reach him—

He amputated the thought. He was sure. The enemy had faulted; perhaps it had been deliberate, and those who had done it were dead or worse.

Siah melted from the circle, loathing burning like spirits. He turned his path in a great arc, weaving along the old road, choosing his path from one second to the next. He wanted to damage the enemy, not deliver his sister's acquiescence. He fingered the blade at his thigh, then the revolver with its two pitiful rounds. It wasn't enough to damage them, even if he had been feeling suicidal.

But the wanting to hurt them would not vanish. He rubbed his face as he meandered, thinking of their Hold, deep in the wastes, even as he sought value in the debris. Not much could be found on the numbered routes anymore: brittle grass had consumed the pavement and the car bodies were useless rust and sun-fractured plastic. Once, they had found books, or preserved electronics in the wrecks. But those days were gone.

A break appeared ahead: an old fuel station, its roof fallen in over the pumps. Siah knew the petroleum had long been salvaged from the ground, but he changed path anyway, pulling out his knife. Maybe he would carve his name with the others on the flaking painted wall, or maybe he would loop around, cutting the long grass as he went.

He was twenty feet from the wall when the first ripple coursed through his senses. His vision crisped. Instinctively, he dove behind a car husk, a metallic scent flooding his nose and tongue, his heart squeezing. He cursed as he waited. The ripple was a foreshock. Somewhere in time ahead, probabilities had shifted. Something unlikely would occur, and the shift, destroying alternative futures, propagated as a shock in space and time.

Siah tried to breathe deep and slow, but his panic had legs under it. This was how it started. Always, a precursor. Foreshocks had come before every time he'd made a quantum switch. And every time, it had ended badly. His thoughts scrambled for his sister. Her face, her voice, her calm. He squeezed his knife hilt until his knuckles cracked, making himself be still. Be calm. And wait.

Two more foreshocks rolled through, but each was less intense. Siah stayed as long as he dared in one place, and nothing more came. Perhaps the probability had diminished. Perhaps, he had beaten it.

He rose and stepped out.

His foot had not touched ground when causality upended. Instantly, Siah left the ninety-six. His feet met earth below an old city tower, rising raggedly skywards from its shed concrete skin. Acid burned his throat. Oh no …

Reality reversed; he was back beside the car husk, striking off towards the city, beginning the journey after it had ended. *Reversi.* Siah's mind whirled with a helpless, unvoiceable scream. The tower appeared again, then he was somewhere between: an old mall, and this time walking backwards. Siah collapsed internally; the nausea crested while the anomaly bent his senses. But his body was not in control. Back and forth, the reversi dragged him, accelerating between states like a spun coin at momentum's end. The sky ripped. Then Siah saw the towers as they had been before the Event: smooth columns lit from within. These were ghosts of past futures. Impossibilities for this world.

Then abruptly, it ended.

The reversi dumped Siah by the mall ruins, their familiar, vine-clad walls blocking out a chunk of night sky. He tripped backwards on a broken pavement and fell on his side, barely missing a great sinkhole, his insides a mess of sensory overload, guilt and fear. He rocked, his watering eyes finding the blurry moon. It had barely moved, though the journey to the mall on foot was at least an hour. Reversi.

Fuck.

In a great heave, he emptied his stomach over the sinkhole's edge, the splash far below. He rolled on his back, holding out his hand to check the shakes. Oh, gods, had he unwritten? Memories surged forward.

He'd surfaced like this once and found the room on fire. It had been the cold dead heart of winter, they'd lived in a salvaged house, with rotten boards like sponges and icy damp inside everything. He'd been dreaming, shivering, wishing it warm. There'd been a pain in his head; he'd woken in the fire, his body convulsing in odd staccato rhythm. His sister had pulled him outside, but their parents had been a floor above. Siah had stood with her, shaking, as the improbable fire melted ice to feed itself, burned sodden boards like no fire should. And finally, he'd seen the fire rings, expanding to the horizon like pond ripples. And the fire was burning snow.

Siah gripped his wrist. His hand kept shaking, but no patterns emerged. *Just the regular terrified shakes.* It wasn't him, not this time. Reversis happened, especially near the old city; everyone knew that. Some of the kids thought it was fun. It scared Siah shitless.

So, it took time to get level. Slowly, he creaked to sitting, his body aching as if he'd been fighting all day. His stomach was a hollow pit, the cold bit his cheeks, the world fuzzy and uncertain around him. The great bulk of the mall ruin was ringed with black sinkholes and crevasses, and bordered with a crumbling, cinderblock wall. After a minute, this wreckage momentarily crisped into hard white lines, as if his sister had brushed him by. Aftershock.

Siah blew out a great breath, and hauled himself together. It was over now. He unfolded the message in his lap, dosing on reality. *Yes*, it said, in quill-scratched ink, *the Seer accepts.* He tapped the paper against his chin, knowing what these four words didn't say. *Accepts a man twice her age, just to make the peace.* She couldn't really want that. *Accepts another Hold, with all their mouths to feed, and just before winter* … she couldn't abide that. He knew her better.

So what was she doing?

Go, brother.

Slowly, Siah got upright. He crept away from the sinkhole and towards the cinderblock wall. He heard *skitter-tink* and his vision tightened. Silence, then a soft *thuck*. Blurry again. A pebble into a sinkhole.

Factors coalesced in Siah's thoughts. This message, the reversi … they bothered him now. This world connected threads you didn't want connected. He frowned and paced, the paper between his fingers.

Go, brother.

She'd had that look in her eye. The one that said she knew what she was doing. She knew he hated peace at this price, that she knew he might disobey … yet, she had sent him.

Siah refolded the note. Did she just expect him to walk into the enemy Hold and hand it over, like he was the defeated? Compromise them all before winter? To look the enemy leader right in the eye and—

Siah stopped, a chill gathering between his ribs. *Look the enemy right in the eye.* She had made him a messenger. *And a messenger could walk right in.* He could come before the enemy leader, easily within strike range.

She had given him a way in.

Siah stuffed the note back in his leathers and scanned the dark wastes, grim but satisfied he had worked it out. Another *skitter-thuck* dyad echoed from the mall, chunks breaking loose from the roof. Siah counted it, and his first problem. His blades and revolver would be no good; the enemy would disarm him at their gate.

He needed a concealable weapon.

He prowled the derelict mallground, intent on a solution, even from this long-since-looted place. He checked behind rubble piles, thick with white bird shit, avoiding the dark corners where wild scents warned him of bear dens. But it was something simple that made him stop.

One wall was soot-splashed from an old fire, and when the breeze lifted his hair, he smelt char, and he remembered. In the first Hold war, before he was of age, the hunters had tapped fuel from underground tanks and stirred it to jelly with white plastic foam. The Hold's Old Man had shown them how.

The stuff had made Siah dizzy, and he'd still been high when they'd loosed it on the enemy. The stuff had burned like unholy fire, scaring him with memories of that icy cabin he told no one about. When they were done, the forest wastes and the enemy had burned to a black pock in the trees.

Siah fingered his water flask. He knew where to look for petroleum; the flask would carry enough charge for the enemy Hold.

He skirted a crevasse, where the pavement had fallen into the underground parking lot, and headed for the mall building. This site had been scavenged over and over, but he could try to find entry into the lot. Sometimes, in the dark, dry corners you could get lucky: find a car with a plastic fuel tank. And if not, he counted a half-dozen other sites to try. He mapped them out in his head, tracing the shortest route, making a plan, confident he could have what he needed by morning.

His back prickled. Siah stopped, a sick feeling replacing confidence. Even under the dappled moon glow, the ruined wall before him was clear, his vision crisp. He waited for the ripple to pass, but it didn't. He knew his mistake. He'd gotten too far ahead, made a goddam *plan* ... that was always when they came. The breeze smelled sweet.

Oh, gods.

Drel. Already here.

His heart heaved as he looked for the monster.

Pressure jacked inside his skull. *Drel!* it said, *Run!*

His eyes tracked through the shadowed holes where cold air huddled, across the crumbling wall nooks and into the edge of the wastes beyond. He wheeled in all directions, waiting for movement to show him what he sought ...

He cursed himself. These were a hunter's tricks: look for the prey in the places it will hide, wait for it to move. But a Drel would do no such things. A Drel saw what was most unlikely, that was its opportunity. So it would lurk where Siah would least look, and it would not betray itself. Probability monsters, exploiting his every weakness.

He looked again.

There it was. Right in the open, crouched atop the jagged line of the wall. Close, and above him.

The moon made a wiry halo of its matted hair, and etched the ropy muscles of its torso. Its fingers clawed the wall edge. Watching, just watching.

Siah had never been so close, and he knew his clear vision meant a certainty chute: in a probabilistic universe, being here with the Drel had escaped likelihood. It was set, no escape, at least while the chute persisted. This was how Drels caught ordinary men.

But Siah was not ordinary. His long-suppressed drive to quantum switch, to unwrite reality, burned his nose. He swallowed convulsively, tasting metal like he'd drunk molten steel.

But the Drel did not move. Siah met its gaze. Intent, purposeful. A once-was-man creature. A thing that stole people to make more of itself. That exploited the universe in a way men could not. Intelligent but mad. Utterly dangerous.

And Siah knew it wanted him to see.

Something fizzed deep in Siah's head, as if his thoughts were the bursting scum on a boiling pot. As the Drel watched, a single idea gathered in the foam. A familiar idea, a desire ... no, an invitation. Siah shifted his weight. The Drel mimicked him, and suddenly they were locked. The idea focused.

Brother.

Siah frowned, pushing on the Drel's thought. It pushed back.

Brother.

Siah recoiled.

The chute broke. The Drel blurred into grays and silvers streaked across the smudged moon. Siah fumbled for his blade, the thought reverberating. *Brother, brother, brother.* Then the wall was empty, the broken moon alone above. The Drel had left him. But it wanted him. Knew him.

Siah fell forward, slashing at the empty air, screaming his rage. No, he was not that! Brick mortar broke between his fingers and he collapsed in a dust-covered crouch. His heart lurched through his ribs. *Brother, brother,* he heard in his head. Persistent, whispering.

Telling.

Siah snatched his blade and pressed the point between his ribs. *No. No. No,* he hissed. The blade cut, and with pain, the panic eased. For all the evils he had done, he was not Drel-kin. Those multiverse fuckers, childstealers, man-eaters!

He. Was. Not. That.

Frantic, he climbed the wall, scanning the wastes, shaking. The forest was a dappled gray sheet, punctured with deep, black holes. Behind, the wrecked mall glowed white between its shadows. No sign of the Drel.

Siah tried to remember his sister's face, but all he could see was Drel-matted hair in the moonlight. His gut curdled. How was he different to them, really? He'd caused the fire that had ended his mother and father. He tried not to think of his daughter, but her eyes had been so like his. Blood on his hands.

His sister had protected him, but she couldn't change what he was. Q-liner. Do-no-gooder. Sometime, he would slip and bad things would come again; not wanting it to happen wouldn't be enough. And the Drels wanted him.

Go, Brother.

The note was a lump in his belt. He dug out the paper, smoothed it out. *The Seer accepts.* She had made him a messenger. Had her knowing look.

Siah swallowed. His earlier assumption had not gone far enough. Yes, she had given him a way in, but she also knew about him. He didn't need a weapon. He could do what no one else could. He could walk into the enemy Hold and unwrite them all. It didn't matter what probabilistic chaos he produced, and long as it destroyed them … and him too. No loose ends, and their own Hold would be safe.

Two ripples coursed through his skull bone, as if his brain were being ripped from the dura. Siah took this as endorsement. He scrambled down, dazed. This was really happening. Would happen.

So, it had come to this.

He paused only a moment. He did not want life to end, but there were worse things. Once, from a distance, he'd seen a man the Drels had taken, one they hadn't killed. He wasn't a man anymore. He'd run, four-legged, fingernails black with old blood, slipping in and out of time. A quantum cheat, a true multiverse creature.

Siah knew the Drel he'd seen would come for him. And when they took him, he wouldn't be just like them, he'd be a Q-liner among them, untroubled by conscience.

Well, fuck that shit.

Siah moved, his hide shoes quiet on the rubble. He was marked. One fate or another would kill him. His sister knew this. His only choice was to go first. He could destroy the enemy and himself more surely than any fire, or he could let the Drels take choice from him.

He ran, his breath ragged, crashing into the forest wastes, dodging the great new trunks and the houses they had eaten. Ripples cut through, strengthening, his sight focused and released, and he struck himself on branches and corners. But even with blood and bruises, the world made way for him, and in some corner of his mind, it seemed beautiful now, in the way all fleeting things do.

Breathless and steaming, he came on the enemy Hold. It was an old school hall, boarded and barricaded, elevated from the shadowy wastes. Siah's thoughts had frayed, his skin puckered with welts. His nose burned, the urge to quantum switch building. He put his arms over his head and half fell into the torchlight, the note crunched in his fist.

Their watch called the warning. Two enemy hunters materialized, wide-eyed and angry, burning torches held high. Siah let them kick him down and strip his blades. They emptied his revolver, click-click, click-click. Burning pitch dripped, its acrid smoke coating his throat. Then he was hauled up and two blade tips dimpled his back.

They asked him something; he missed it. They struck him.

Purpose, they demanded again.

Siah got his tongue moving. *Messenger*, he growled, unfurling his fist to show the crumpled paper, now spotted with blood.

They checked him once more, then shoved him towards the Hold. Candles flickered in the windows like fireflies. News of his arrival would be racing. Brother to sister, mother to son. Enemy to enemy. The burn increased.

Sound assaulted him as they pushed him inside. He fooled himself that he would control what was coming: *not yet, not yet*. The world become a vaulted room, its air rich with torch smoke. The enemy were dark-eyed masses. Siah smelled the hunters: male stink of blood and sweat. They forced him down before a gathered half-circle. Sweat stung his scrapes, his breath shuddered. Dozens of enemy in the room. The burn to switch became a painful focus, now easier to give into than suppress. He thought of fire that climbed walls, bricks that crumbled to dust. Waited only for the right moment to manifest.

And before, the chute would come. Almost …

Then Siah looked the enemy in the face.

Two black eye-blurs in pale disc face. The burn held, teetering. Siah felt the strangest sensation: ripples washing through him, back and forth, in regular rhythm. Something like he experienced when he switched, but stable, not staccato.

His vision cleared fully and his scalp crawled. A man stared back. A battle-scarred face with a broken nose and dark hair. He had six-shooter at his hip, a wolf-pelt across his chest. This was their leader, Siah realized. The one his sister had accepted.

Siah could not switch. He stared, shocked. The man's eyes were creased in deliberate squint. His gaze shifted, but the telltale movements were so suppressed that no one normal would notice. This man was the source of the ripples, of Siah's cleared vision.

Another Q-liner. But a leader, a man in control.

Siah froze solid. The edge of his anger dulled; he had never imagined this possible. Q-liners were killed and exiled; they couldn't lead, couldn't have success. And yet here …

The leader concealed the shock that Siah saw plainly and briefly in his face, but did not pretend. In this moment, they were men to each other.

Siah felt the message in his palm. He finally saw his sister's face again, her knowing look. *Go, brother.*

Slowly, he extended his hand. The paper stuck to his skin, message bound to messenger, four words that had brought him to a new world. *This* was what she had known. He took a single, shuddering breath. For all he had thought, he had not imagined this.

The leader gripped Siah's hand around the paper. Siah felt their calluses meet, a brief contact of alliance forged. Siah looked again and the message was gone.

He slumped, the burn gone, his body spent. He tried not to think of how close this night had come to ending differently. He had expected to unwrite himself into scrambled nothingness. Instead, he was here, and it was done. That his flaw was both destruction and salvation—that was too much to process now. But for the first time, he did not feel alone.

The note passed around the circle; tension eased, the mood warmed. The hunters' faces were relief. Then cheers, a party began. The war was over.

Siah and the leader were alone in the thick of it. Siah found himself kneeling, the night ending as it had begun. The leader pulled him up. A strong grip, a direct blue stare. They were the same height, carried the same weight.

"Your name," said the leader, offering his hand.

Siah thought a long time, then took it.

"Brother," he said.

ALCHEMY & ICE

Shortlisted for the Aurealis Award for Best Science Fiction Story

Cold is the language of the world now, its syllables snow and frost and ice. City towers crumble white and gray, the backdrop sky rinsed pale blue, the pavements sunk with indigo pools. But life is a warm thing, like steam and embers. Red, vermillion, orange. Colors now bled from the everyday, reserved for the Steam Daemon alone. And so nothing speaks like the flush of life in the palate of this algid city.

That is how Fortescue finds The Soldier in the snow, her cheeks tinted with the last of her body's heat. Under her cloak her uniform is rags, snow cams in white and smudge and charcoal. A soldier like him, frozen on patrol. Another unit's field hands, far from home, and in the forbidden quarter, just as he is.

Neither of them should be here.

He can no longer see the path she's taken; all above and around covered in white, the steely sky promising more. He knows from that building, on that angle, that the great sinkhole is near, and he debates the wisdom of leaving her. Sometimes, the cold and desperate try for the heartland of the Steam Daemon, go mad for its reverse mirage, tendrils of heat rising from the deep, promising a thaw. But if the frost doesn't claim them, the crawlies will. If either is her fate, his thick heart has a beat of sympathy. But only one.

He unclenches his hands from his weapon and reaches for her tattered cloak. Probably she will die. Never awaken from the snow-cold slumber. The pump in his chest keeps its ragged pace; she is nothing to him. This is nothing to him.

Dragging her loose sets her flailing, and a shivering wracks her limbs as she flings herself confusedly forth. He has to use his weight on her shoulders, sharp bones under his hardened hands. And when he's wrapped her in his issued cloak, with its captain's pips stitched in faded red like her cheeks, she resists him, making to run on legs that cannot support her. She dives back into the snowdrift, shifting frantic flurries like an animal. She is mad, then. He should leave her to wander here until the cold and crawlies claim her end.

Then she drags a limp corpse from the drift.

He stumbles back, falls, the shock sharp as the tundra on the seat of his pants. In her white fingers is the coarse black fur he sees in his worst dreams. A giant rat-like thing, its face deformed, features cast sideways under a heavy blow. Thick, torn ears. Copper-pressed teeth. A rent has opened in its side, spilling thick grease and loose cogs. Its fur is crowned with a welder-tip tail, now kinked and spark-less.

Crawlie.

Even dead, it shoots panic into his frozen muscles. It is an agent of the Daemon infecting the city's pipes and boilers. Chasers, harassers and disappearers of men. Fortescue has only once seen one this close, and has never seen one dead. He didn't know they could die.

He drags his gaze to The Soldier's half-frozen face. In the ten years of war, the resistance has wanted this, and never had it. A chance to know the enemy. To find weakness.

Now, she holds such a chance.

A tiny patch of color blooms on his blue heart. Pale red, like her cheeks, like the insignia of his rank. Like hope.

With his arm under her shoulder, he drags her back to the line he should not have crossed, the exclusion around the sinkhole, that creeps outwards every year. He carries the crawlie in his fist, its broken internals shifting as he swings his arm. The weight of it unnerves him, draws a splinter of memory that he plucks before it can grow. He tries to see it for what it is: a fur bag of cog-driven grease soup, made to serve the Daemon. A thing that inch by inch has taken his life, until all that remains in him is the soldier.

Back on safer ground, he pulls them into an abandoned concrete crevice and pulls a precious vial of blue fire from his pocket. Three drips set a wet log burning, a slim, illicit flame sending its smoke into a catching roof. Later, when he is long gone, the smoke will leak skywards and the crawlies will come. For now, Fortescue throws the dead one onto the snowdrift. SentryOne, the best crawlie cat, hisses from the shadows as he lays the woman afore the fire. The hiss is partly from the smell of crawlie, and partly remonstration for being left behind, a decision Fortescue allowed no choice in. He'll risk his own ass, but SentryOne is too important to fall in a border violation. Soon, the cat is sniffing around the dead crawlie.

"Leave it," rumbles Fortescue. SentryOne bats the misshapen face with his claw.

The Soldier wraps her arms around her legs, her cheekbones hills atop her too-thin face. Fortescue looks closer. Her regiment patch is defunct; two seasons old, at least. She has been gone a long time. Long enough for a deserter. This knowledge thickens the silence as they thaw.

"Do I take you back?" he asks her. "Or do you want to run?"

She turns up her chin, glances at her prize. A piece of the enemy, hard won. He sees blood clotted at her neck now, and red welts over her arms returning with her circulation. She peels the cloak from her shoulder. Her rank stares back, far above him, taking his breath, snapping his fingers to his temple.

"Take me to command," she says.

And her voice is pure and clear, ringing in his blushing heart like a snow-cleaned bell.

The guards take her roughly at the barracks gate, more roughly than they need to. Fortescue knows what they are thinking: of the crawlie-swarm that claimed the last safe place, two seasons before. A dead crawlie is more than enough to invoke the memory.

But she marches between them as if they have welcomed her,

her back straight, her bearing proud. Fortescue watches her go, SentryOne curled about his shoulder. He is dismissed. But he knows he will be called to answer questions soon and knows not what he will say. His fingernails scratch through SentryOne's fur, comforted by the cat's insides, bone and blood, not grease and gear.

He treks to his bunk, in the frosty barrack hall, and closes his eyes with the furry puddle between his hands. An unfamiliar feeling chases itself around his guts: he wonders how the truth might hurt her: finding her in the forbidden zone like that. And he doesn't know why he should have such a thought.

They wake him to answer before he is really asleep. A panel of them, majors and above in the best of threadbare uniforms. She is there, too. Sitting where she has been told, to the side like a prisoner, though she ranks as high as they do. The crawlie prize stretches atop a center table, like an accusation.

"Captain Fortescue," begins the Major. "You will tell us your version."

Fortescue doesn't know what she has told them, but when he looks at her, he knows she has not the bearing for lies. So he tells them he found her in a snowdrift with the captured beast, that he warmed her and brought her back. He leaves out details of where, exactly, no need to admit freely what's worth licks and discharge.

The Major's brows descend, but they do not press, not when the alchemists are straining to get at the prize. Fortescue is sent to the mess, to be fed what meagers can be had. In the wood-lined hall, he will look for Fingle and Bobs, two alchemists who drift together. They try not to call each other friends. Friends are things of the past-world. Now, there are allies and enemies. The ones who help you survive, and the ones who will help themselves.

Fortescue knows, somewhere in the cold heart of him, that the panel are deciding which one applies to The Soldier in the snow. He should not care about this. She is not part of his orders. But something of her has stuck with him, resting on his soul like a snowflake.

Fingle and Bobs are not in the mess and soon Fortescue climbs the stair to the tower watch, huddled with another sentry under the Steam Daemon's night. This kid's been here only a month, cheeks child-soft. But his eyes are specks of flint as they search the snowdrifts for crawlie signs—tracks or furrows, a movement in the shadows, things that freeze an ordinary man with fear. Their gaze returns to the sinkhole's distant plume, again and again. Sometimes, on the clear nights, they can see the glow of coals reflected in the city towers. Fortescue latches his mind on the zone around the sinkhole; it is where he escaped a long-ago death, where he lost all things … and since, a pilgrimage he's made many times. But now, it's where he found The Soldier, his damnation turned would-be salvation. He imagines pitching the blue fire into the depths.

Bone-frozen later, when he retires from the watch to seek dreams of melting ice, a hand catches him at the foot of the stair. Bobs, his face etched with strain, draws him to an alcove where the last of the alchemist's oven heat lingers. Amongst the fumes of black powder and acrid smoke, the smell of the roasting beds that produce the blue fire, Fingle waits for them both.

"You've never seen anything like it," says Fingle, sucking an illicit half-smoke.

"Yes," nods Bobs. "Animal and machine, induction powered through the tail. If it wasn't so broken, it would probably try to haul itself away."

Fortescue shudders. He's re-lived the swarm that should have claimed him every night, but now these memories are tangled with the days just past. So he asks them about The Soldier in the snow.

"In the cell block," says Bobs but dismissively. He shakes Fortescue by the hand, thanks for what he has brought. "Well done, man. The tail is not much damaged. We are trying to repair it. We are hopeful."

Fortescue's temper warms his core. He shakes off Bobs. To be in the cells, The Soldier is suspected, even after she has brought them this prize. He bets she is hungry, thirsty. And for the first time, he thinks more of her than of what his actions might mean for the resistance.

He takes SentryOne and his uneaten rations, and slips through the barracks to the cell block. The moon is full tonight, filtered behind the steely gray sky. The ill-fed guard is asleep, never stirring as Fortescue finds her.

She sits against the wall, striped in the pale bars of light. SentryOne purrs with cool breath, and Fortescue wraps his hands around the cold cell steel.

"How did you do it?" he asks. "How did you kill one, and bring it back?"

She rises and glides closer, ever closer, so that her voice will not carry. "To tell you such would be a long story," she says. "But you know it ends here, and that is enough."

"You were sent a long time ago."

"Two years," she says.

Knowledge passes unsaid between them. Two years. She is from the barracks that was lost, then, the one overrun.

His voice is a rumbling whisper. "Sent or taken?"

She closes her eyes, and he sees the fight in her; the want to tell him things that she can never tell. Classified things. Things she has done in the name of their cause. Risk and suffering and sacrifice.

He shakes his head, speaks the simple truth. "Don't say it. You outrank me." These words are coated in the awe he feels for her. More a soldier than he is.

She searches his face and he sees every cross of her eyelashes. "I am nothing," she says. "What I brought is the prize."

"They are working on it."

Her expression flickers, and for the first time, he sees doubt in her. "I tried to warn them," she says. "Do they know what they are doing?"

Do they know what they are doing?

Fortescue has never questioned it before. He is a soldier. He has superiors, a chain of command. He came here when there was nowhere else to go. The resistance has many like him, but the alchemists are of higher learning. Clever men, fighting this war with them. And now, they have all they need—an advantage—don't they?

Don't they?

They question him again as the sun is rising, a weak pale streak through the heavy sky. Snow is coming again. Fortescue feels it deep in his marrow, a sense honed from months of patrolling in the Steam Daemon's lee. But now, he feels his confidence slipping, as if he is a lone rock in the spring, all the snow receding to leave him stranded, exposed.

"Tell us your story again," says the Major.

So he tells it, same as before. They are satisfied this time. But only with him.

"We find no record of her mission," says the Major. "Which means at best it was not endorsed. But we must also entertain the worst: the possibility she is a fraud. An infiltrator. An agent herself of the Daemon."

Fortescue hears this, but not as he might have before. He knows that in two years the command structure has turned over, that records have been lost to snowmelt and mildew, that the mood of the group is volatile. He sees the fear in them, the way it bends their words; they know not what to do with her. Easier if she is a danger; they know what to do with those.

For the first time, their mood cannot infect him. He has felt what it was like to pull her from the snow, to see her duty followed through. Her resolve in the face of immeasurable risk. Because of these things, she will not leave him, a colored spot in the monochrome of his thought and feeling. And so in turn, he will not leave her to uncertain fate.

Bobs wakes Fortescue from an uneasy slumber, where dreams have been of crackling footsteps on the thin skin of a crevasse.

"They have fixed it," says Bobs. And nothing more. But Fortescue hears doubt, and Bobs does not head back to the lab. Instead, he takes the bend at the end of the hall, towards the alchemist quarters he shares with Fingle, a backward glance inviting Fortescue to follow.

He pulls a sleeping SentryOne against his chest, but his bones ache with portent, and the cat's claws dig into his neck. The first snow whispers down as he reaches the alchemists' doorway. Bobs braces his hands on the chamber's open window sill.

"What?" asks Fortescue.

Bobs rakes a hand through his hair. "I think we should have waited."

"Why?"

"We don't understand enough."

Fortescue has never heard an alchemist doubt before. His teetering world tips its last edge. The snow will melt. And he will not sleep again until the night has passed into a new morning.

She is waiting by the bars, head turned as if listening. He sees the turmoil inside him reflected in her eyes, that she shares the fear the world is about to fall under their feet.

He braces his hands against the bars. "How was a senior rank approved to go into the field?" he asks her.

Her silence tells him that she was never approved. Then she says, "I was an experiment. A volunteer."

Fortescue nods; it must have been so. His voice finds the quiet between their heartbeats. "You were not expected to survive."

"No."

"But you found a way." He swallows. "Are you one of the Daemon's?" He asks as though there is a chance: that he can extricate himself, forget her if she is part of the enemy, even though he knows it is futile.

"I am not. But I learned how to survive there. How to be useful; trade myself for their purpose. I learned their signals … pipe, wall and skin, it's all the same. How the Daemon thinks. How it uses every chance to starve us out. How it chooses its moments." Her eyes flit and she shudders. "I am changed."

As the flakes gather silent around his feet, he asks, "Did you intend to die in the snow?"

"It would perhaps have been for the best," she says. "The Daemon would not have allowed me leave without a plan of its own. I turned back, so many times. Each step made the risk seem too great. I sat on the drift. I meant for the cold to take my choice. Then when I woke, I remembered what it was like to be here. Why I had gone to begin with."

Warmth trickles inside Fortescue's chest. There is a cant in her words, a tiny nod of possibility that he changed her decision to die.

He shakes it off, angry at himself. She would never allow such a weakness.

Her eyes harden into ice chips. "I had hoped that the alchemists had learned these years. That they would know this is an enemy that thinks just as they do. I needed them to be that smart. I tried to warn them."

Fortescue's teeth grind. He is a silent soldier, one who's seen how the command structure works. The hunger for knowledge to one-up the enemy—that's what drives the officers. They would not have listened to caution from someone they did not know. "The alchemists are under command, now, more than ever," he says. "They do what they are bid."

She sighs, silent for a thought-strung moment before she speaks. "They should not have reactivated the drone." Fortescue sees now how her fingers rest on the bars, the longest three like soft antennas.

His bones carry frost into his heart. SentryOne leaps from his shoulders and streaks the hall, a running shadow on high alert. For Fortescue feels now through the floor what she has felt with her fingertips, what SentryOne detects with his whiskers. The dozens of running feet, through pipe and sewer and every crawlspace.

The Soldier's skin is moonlit pale, the despair of home lost writ in the pull of her cheek. They are an island afore a wave, now. Fortescue knows he has reached a cusp he never knew existed. The one where he chooses his fate, and hers too. Perhaps the last decision he can ever make. He takes the keys from the sleeping guard and opens her door. "Wait here," he says.

Fingle and Bobs have the freezing fear, clutching their quarters' doorway. They already know what everyone does. Crawlies are coming. No one will leave alive. But Fortescue has survived once; he knows it's possible with two things: fire, and a way out.

He grabs Fingle and Bobs. "Where do they keep the blue fire?"

But they are not soldiers who can act with fear in their veins. He has to shake them. "Where!"

A single finger points to the alchemists' rugged stair. Fortescue scrambles down the dim recess, lit on the wicks of blue fire lamps.

The lab is bare, but for the cold, coal-fire bed, and the paltry rack of precious vials, holding the blue fire, a clear liquid like fresh melted snow. All they have. He dumps every one into a flask, the vapors bending his senses, numbing his fingertips. He hopes it is enough.

Fingle and Bobs are pressed against the wall when he rises from the stair. The whole barracks has fallen into quiet: the silence of hiding, of concealment, of attempted survival. Fortescue knows it won't be enough.

He grabs their collars and hauls them to the cell block, with its wooden floor. They can hear the swarm, now. Scratching steps that scuttle and search. Then a shape leaps onto Fortescue's back, and the nightmare terror lances through his neck. He spins to slam the crawlie against the wall, then hears the hiss in his ear.

"Goddamn it, SentryOne."

The cat only digs his claws in harder, as if he's holding tight for the only way out.

The Soldier is waiting by the bars, a silhouette in the moon's pale glow.

Unnaturally calm. "You should not do this," she says.

Fortescue throws wide her cage. He can think of nothing else; she is in his thoughts the way the cold enters on a winter's night. "The fort is lost," he says.

"And we are trapped." She casts an eye at Fingle and Bobs, who have slumped shivering against the cage.

He shakes his head, even as the scampering echoes down the long hall. He kicks the guard's stool to show the trapdoor into the cellar.

"Going to ground is worse. They leave nothing behind," she says. But still, she pushes Fingle and Bobs to the door, and down into the darkness. Fortescue snatches the flask of blue fire and sloshes it across the hall end. The wood smolders, a hell-fire heat rising from the slick. He sees them then; the racing snouts filling the walls and floor.

"Come on," he begs the blue fire.

With a *woomph!* it catches, blowing Fortescue against the cage. He rolls for the trapdoor as the fire consumes the hall. He falls, his knee taking the stone-hard jar.

He pushes up, through air thick with cold. They must get out before crawlies find a way in, through drain or pipe. And before the blue fire spreads like unholy wind.

The cellar ladder rises into the outside world, the grate frozen in place. Fortescue shoves it with his shoulder, feeling tendons stretch and pop. He sends the others ahead of him, out into the snowdrifts under the midnight sky. Only now they are outside can they hear the shrieks. But they are clear. A chance. As if hope is too much, he stumbles and cannot rise again. His knee is finished; shoulder, finished. "Go. Run!" he yells.

The alchemists vanish into the snowy night, but The Soldier stays. His heart wrenches with the lost chance of knowing her more. "Go," he begs.

But she is under his good arm, hauling upwards. He struggles. "You'll never move fast enough if you help."

But she will not abide him giving up, will not leave him behind. He understands this, even as he hates it. They are soldiers first. Everything else second.

They stumble through the snowdrift; it is too easy to see where Fingle and Bobs have gone. They will be followed. So she hauls him towards the broken high-ground where the asphalt and grass are dim and snowless.

"There's a sealed refuge this way," he gasps between breaths. But he can feel SentryOne's claws tightening, the feral hiss building inside the cat. The crawlies are on their tail.

They fight on until the mouth of an alley where SentryOne's hiss becomes audible. The Soldier stops. Turns his face to her with the flats of her hands. "You pulled me from the snow," she says. He sees the glint in her eyes. She thinks she owes him.

"Don't," he says, desperate. "Take SentryOne and go on ahead. Bobs and Fingle—they need you. Command needs you." *I need you.*

Her smile is sad. She glances over her shoulder. "I lived in their tunnels for two years," she said. "I can give you time."

A sickly horror grips Fortescue about the gut. "No."

Her face turns cold, all but her cheeks in their blooming red. "That's an order, soldier. Go."

Fortescue has never broken his heart before, but it does right there under the frost-flaked sky. "I won't leave you," he says.

"Then I must leave you." She kisses him swiftly, a tiny ring of heat on his chilled cheek, and whispers a leaving into his ear.

Then she is gone into the Steam Daemon's night, too swift for a lame man to follow. Fortescue wants to holler after her, but the cavern in his chest claims his voice. And instead, with no choice, he hauls himself towards the refuge. The night rings with the screech of crawlies, louder and louder until he is shut inside.

In the aching cold, he strikes a supply match, a single bloom of heat in the dark.

Three faces, three survivors.

And as he waits, he hears the words she whispered.

I survived once. I will again. I will find you when the snow melts.

ARACHNE

Before he served the carbon age, Tobias was a spy. That brief career began under the heavy hand of his uncle, who ran the Grim Maiden iron foundry on the banks of the Thames. Toby's first job was shoveling coal into the feed chute for the Maiden's tethered dragon, an enormous indentured beast with red-black scales and broken flapping ears, who ate coal and shat ashes and melted iron with its breath. As he humped the black rocks to and fro, Toby avoided looking in the dragon's eye, for it revealed a melancholy beast with sour disposition. Even black-handed and lowly, Toby hoped he was not destined for a similar fate.

He took steps to ensure it. He hid papers in his pockets marked the *Royal Academy*, smudge-marked and dog-eared, but lovingly read over and over. He'd found them deep in his uncle's bin, but this, and his aspirations to leave the Grim Maiden forever, were two things he never revealed. As his uncle tirelessly reminded, these were difficult times.

For the Grim Maiden stared across the river at the Spinning Jenny carbon factory, edifice to edifice, great competitors, both supplying steam-harnessing boilers and pipes. But while the Grim Maiden worked in fine iron and steel, the Spinning Jenny wove theirs from black carbon thread and resin, which put his uncle in dangerous blue funk.

"This carbon!" he declared, gesticulating as he paced just out of reach of the dragon, mustache quivering in time with his vast belly. "It's no match for steel in the joints you see, but they'll solve that soon enough. I was cheated in this damn deal. Damn those Academy men!"

Toby's senses tweaked at the mention of the Academy and a *deal*, but he hovered uncomfortably with a half-shovel of coal, knowing one of the stolen Academy papers (on the evolution of higher species using transalimentary tinctures) was protruding from his pocket. He had seen the Spinning Jenny boilers being floated down the river, so light they could be moved by a single man, and with the black criss-cross allure visible through their transparent skins. The Grim Maiden tanks frequently broke the axles of delivery carts. Toby knew this because he'd been reading his uncle's papers, late at night, when the factory was quiet. He also suspected, from yellowed correspondence, old invoices and hints in the man's diary, that the Spinning Jenny and his uncle had once been partners.

All this he kept firmly to himself. His uncle was a clever man, but with a vein of intractable cruelty, like a smoky line in quartz. Tobias often caught the dragon, who was regularly on the end of the lash, sizing the man up with a murderous eye.

So, now, Toby didn't know whether to keep moving and be shouted at for not listening, or listen and be shouted at for not working.

His uncle leaned in close, fingering the paper hanging from Toby's pocket. "What do you think, boy?"

Caught, Toby's stomach flamed like a furnace. "About what?"

"Think you're clever, don't you, boy? Are you working for the Spinning Jenny? Did you help them take my business? Answer me!"

Toby's thumping pulse beat his throat closed. He watched a sweat drop track across tangled veins at his uncle's temple. Did his uncle know about him taking the papers?

"Lucky," his uncle said a moment later, wiping the sweat into his greasy mustache. "A guilty man always protests innocence. Still, this habit of overreaching your station must be stamped out. More work, that's the answer. Useful work."

His uncle acquired a thoughtful expression, then leant down again, his hot rank breath swirling into Toby's face. His knuckles creaked as he seized Toby's collar. "The Spinning Jenny's looking for a new floor lad. I need to know what they're doing over there, you hear? And they don't know who you are. You'll go. And report to me each day."

Toby could scarce believe his luck. Out from under his uncle and the dragon. Into the world beyond the Grim Maiden. He snatched up the shovel and gaily hoicked coal into the chute.

"Oh, boy?" said his uncle.

"Yes?" said Toby.

His uncle pointed to the dragon. "You cross me, that's where you're going for breakfast."

The next morning, Toby became a spy.

He found differences between the two factories quickly. The Spinning Jenny was not sooty like the Grim Maiden, but covered in a layer of soft fibrous down. Toby turned the stuff through his fingers, until he discovered this led to a fearful itch that was unabated by scratching. This was unfortunate, because Toby's official role was gathering up masses of the black fluff for deposit into a giant hopper.

The source of the black fiber was the thing that stole Toby's attention. A great mechanical spider, her body panels of beaten brass and studded steal, gleaming under the gas lamps. Her legs worked her spinnerets in a blurred fury, while two pasty, dumb, resurrectionist-crafted workers spooled the fine thread onto reels for the winders. Toby swept distractedly, watching the spinnerets work, until the Academy men moved him on. These men were always before her, dressed in waistcoats and top-hats, and holding up great cards before her dull red-lens eyes. Toby snuck a look at the cards and found them covered in complex mathematics, which he tried to memorize for later comparing to his papers.

Adjoining the spider's weaving room was the winder room, where a series of colossal machines ran from a great crank shaft, which itself emerged with a good deal of steam and dirt spray, through the floor. The winders pulled the threads off their spools and passed them through a dripping resin tray, before a turning shaft laid the wet fibers down on a wax mandrel.

One mandrel was huge and boiler shaped, while the others were long and narrow for pipes. The threads wrapped around until the whole surface was covered, then the machine kept a creeping rotation while the resin set hard as glass. Toby worked this out by experimental poking of the windings in various stages of set, at which he was caught at twice, once copping a sock to the ear, and another the threat of expulsion, a fact he concealed from his uncle. Besides, his uncle only wanted to know about the spider.

"I don't care for their damned winder-bobbits!" he declared. "For I could make one myself with any engineer competent in industrial thievery! No, boy, I want to know of the source of the carbon-fiber, that great arachnid. She is the key. And I want her stopped, do you hear?"

"But uncle, the science men are always with her. And they chase me away."

"Well, then, you're no good to me at all, and I'd just as sooner have you sunk in the river."

This exchange bore new consequences. His uncle raved long into the evening, pacing by the glowing forge fire, just beyond the reach of the dragon, muttering about wrongs and slights and promises broken.

Keeping one ear on his uncle's raving, Toby snuck into the study and read more crinkling pages of the man's diary. He discovered his uncle had once been party to the Academy. But the entries of formulae and complaints about Kelvin only comprised a few pages, ended abruptly, and there began the problems. Someone had crossed Toby's uncle, and the scratchy madman writing hinted both at the rage that followed, and that definitive action had been taken.

Toby put the diary aside with a churning in his guts. His uncle already knew he was reading papers. He'd better attempt to stop the spider or he might become cinders for the dragon's forge, or a deadweight at the bottom of the river.

He tried the following night. He affected extra slowness, and worked his way into the spider's room right near the shift's end. Standing behind a wide steam pipe, he was missed in the final check. A half-hour later, the factory was silent. Toby poured cold tea into a china cup reserved for the Academy men, imagining himself critiquing Lord Kelvin, and worked on some kind of plan.

As a first attempt at sabotage, he upended half the cup of tea into the resin bath of one of the winding machines. There, he could convincingly tell his uncle he'd tampered with their formula.

Sipping on the last of the evidence, Toby sidled round the wall towards the spider's head. It was beautiful, really, but menacing. Delicately curled against a little platform, supported by a plinth, legs curled in multi-jointed archways, except for the two slowly cycling at the spinnerets. The resurrectionist-workers, chained, vacant-eyed and slack-jawed, only had to twitch the fiber once each minute. The two of them gave Toby the creepy-skin wiggins, but it was the spider he was really wary of. She looked as though she would scurry after him if he turned his back. He wasted a good turn of the clock scaring himself with spider-chasing scenarios. He wasn't sure what was worse; his imaginings what she might do to him, or that he was expected to destroy something so magnificent.

Toby inched up the railed walkway. This was where the Academy men always stood to hold up the formula cards. He looked about for the creamy sheets—his uncle would be impressed with one of those—but none remained.

The only thing on the platform was a short length of pipe. Toby was still unsure whether the spider was automata—gears and springs and alchemist's secrets—or dynamo powered. Still, the pipe was thick and would equally disrupt cog or spark.

Toby surveyed the beast. Her panels were smooth like armor, and he'd have to climb to reach anything other than her head, where six dull red eyes stared lifeless from their oversized sockets, two larger than the rest. Otherwise the face was featureless, but for a pinched circle orifice in the lower third. Screwing up his face in distaste, Toby shoved the pipe up this opening, where it smartly jammed, protruding two inches. Toby tried shoving it further to no avail. Oh dear. That would certainly be noticed.

And worse, nothing appeared to change.

Desperate, but losing will for destruction, Toby emptied the pitiful remains of his tea into one of the spider's eye sockets. The liquid was barely a few drops, so he threw in the cup after it. Toby waited until he heard the end of its thumping descent. There!

Surely, that would do some ill. Toby scurried off to report what he considered success.

His uncle was unimpressed. "And did yer stay to ensure she stopped in her spinning, did you, boy?"

Toby's ass smarted in anticipation. "N-no. She wasn't really spinning anyway, uncle. Not when the Academy men aren't there!"

"Git back there an' make sure!"

It occurred to Toby that he might simply escape his uncle by applying himself to his job at the Spinning Jenny, but the idea was too fresh to gain traction. Instead, he allowed himself to snivel on the way back.

The factory's insides were black on black, and Toby kept running into fiber-coated surfaces. By the time he reached the spider's room, he was scratching like a flee-ridden ape. The spider seemed quieter, until he heard a low hum, and noticed her eyes glowed dull red, reflecting dimly across every surface. The pipe he'd jammed in her head was still there.

Mmmmmmmmmmmm.

God, was one of the resurrectionist-workers loose? Toby stood up on the railing to check, and found himself looking straight into the spider's eye. He wondered what had become of the tea cup.

"Mmmmmmmmmmmooooooo."

Toby froze. The hum ran through the railing and up his hands; the source was close. He peered around. The workers were in their places. Was someone else here?

"Hello?" he called feebly. He tried to think of a story to explain what he was doing, should he indeed be caught. He pretended to brush fibers off the spider's head.

"Mmmmmmooooooorrrrr."

Toby jerked and nearly fell, the hum dancing in his fingers. It came from the spider's head!

"Mmmooorre," said the vibration.

"More?" asked Toby.

"Eeeeeesssss."

Toby hung off the railing, frozen as he listened. The voice was high and tinny, as though someone was *in* the spider's head speaking down the tube. The Spinning Jenny's owner had a daughter who sometimes appeared in the office window, corseted and trimmed in Kevlar-patterned fabric. Toby crawled to the top railing to peer deep inside the eye cavity, looking for blonde ringlets and the grin of an executed prank ... but he could see nothing, not even the tea cup. Just the dull red glow. The cavity was too small for a person.

"Oooooorrrtaaaa," insisted the spider-voice.

Orta? Orta? Toby mouthed the sounds.

"*Ooowwwwaaaattaaaa.*"

"Oh! Water!"

"Eeeesssss. Mmmooorre. Owatttaaa."

Toby looked about. The Royal Academy men were always the ones who attended the spider, and he'd never seen them feed her. But the spider was speaking to him. She needed water. Maybe they'd forgotten before they left.

He could find no cup, but the wash-down bucket by the wall was half-full of rank soapy liquid, a quarter inch of grease on top. Toby supposed it would do. He slopped the lot into the spider's eye cavity, getting at least half on himself.

Abruptly the vibration lost its tinniness, and the spider-voice oiled and smoothed.

"Anku. Elp me."

"Help you ... what?" said Toby.

"Ankyou fooor elping me."

"Oh, you're welcome," said Toby, brushing his lapels proudly. He was like an Academy man. Spider tender. Definitely *not* something to mention to his uncle. He frowned at the thought. What would he tell his uncle now?

He stepped down, lower lip in his teeth.

"Wait."

Toby stopped. The spider seemed to fix him with her dull red eyes, legs curled, except the two nearest the spinnerets, which still slowly cycled. He shivered.

"Help me," she said. Imploring.

He wavered, his uncle playing on his mind. "With what?"

"Three thinngs oaan-leee," said the spider reasonably, her voice better and better. "Say you will, and I will help you."

Toby peered at the tube. One of his papers talked of resonant frequencies. He wondered if the spider was using the pipe so to make the voice. He wanted to know how the water changed the tone. He wanted to study it, like an Academy man. Maybe she would let him.

"All … right," he said.

"Releeese the dragon," she said.

"What?"

"I seeee you at the factory across the water," said the spider. "You can get to the dragon. Releeese it." Toby snuck a look at the narrow wall window through which he could just see the fires of the Grim Maiden foundry. So, the dragon could see. She knew about him. He was *discovered*. He bit his lip, considering which was the greater beast: the spider, or his uncle.

The one in front of him won. Still, Toby coughed in miserable self-pity as he re-entered the Grim Maiden. This was not what he had imagined. Maybe he should just go to bed … but then what would he do tomorrow?

His uncle was asleep at his desk, one hand on his whip, the other inside his pants. The dragon slumbered by the furnace mouth, the low coals reflected as orange smudges on its dull scales. The beast was tethered by two thick chains that ran in opposite directions to two equally thick girders, secured by drop-pins. Toby found the first had rusted solid, but the second was directly below the oil-dripping flywheel for the forge hammers and came away with greased ease. The chain clattered to the floor. The dragon opened one murderous eye. Its gaze noted the flaccid chain, then again found Toby. It rose.

With a wetness in his pants, Toby ran. He didn't stop until he reached the Spinning Jenny and shimmied back inside. The spider's red eyes were fixed across the river. Toby watched, heart racing, until a burst of flame erupted from the Grim Maiden, spinning roof tiles skyward like war-parade confetti. The fire and destruction quickly spread as the dragon – now trailing its two chains – laid waste to the factories across the river. Debris soon clattered on the Spinning Jenny's roof.

Thud, thud, thump.

"Won't the dragon come here, too?" asked Toby.

"Yeeees," rumbled the spider. "Now, undooo those bolts."

"Which?"

She ballerina-ed her legs to point to two bolts, each the size of Toby's arm, which attached a metal loop over her body to the plinth beneath.

"Er," said Toby, sensing the situation was well out of control.

"It is toooo late for second thoughtsss," said the spider silkily. "The Grim Maiden is no more. You are meant for bigger things. You will correct the wrongs of your uncle. These body prisons. Those experimenters. Releeeese me."

"Er, ah ..."

"If you do not, the dragon will find you," she urged. "I will protect you. Releeese me."

Toby considered two things. The dragon was a hideous force, and there was no shortage of coal in the London factories. It would eat and destroy for as long as it wanted. This, and the spider had mentioned his uncle. How did she know him?

It took a good deal of grease-infested maneuvering, but Toby managed the bolts after standing on the end of a shifter bigger than he was. The last nut fell below the plinth with a boom. The bolts were too heavy to remove, but the spider rose up on her spindly legs and pulled both from their holes. She shook once, and the whole shackle tumbled undone. She whipped around her body, stretching her hideous length, glowing red eyes clamped on Toby. His primal center screamed to run. She was too fast to be automata! Too smooth for electrics!

"What are you!" he blurted.

The spider drew back. "I was once a woman of the Academy. This factory was my home. I wove carbon, and my hussssband engineered the furnaces and engines across the river. Brothers owned the factories, men of the Academy. Then the Grim Maiden ... your unnncle ... he accused my husband and I of spying for each other. Convinced the Academy we were traitors, and could be punissshed."

A long silence fell, until Toby thought she had finished. Then, she spoke again, softly as her voice would allow.

"The Academy were experimenting with pressure-moved automata. Hot-oil hydraulics. But they had nothing to drive it. The resurrectionists could not provide intelligence. They needed a living brain. So, they took my body away and put my mind inside *this*."

She shivered her legs, as if repulsed. Toby's mouth hung open. He'd aspired to the Academy, and his mind tore between fascination, and the horror of the methods she described. He was just smart enough to mention neither.

"What happened?" he said instead.

The spider gazed at the cross-river destruction. "I refused. I would not weave the carbon thread for their tanks and boilers and pipes; parts for their new steam engines. So they used extortion. I thought my husband had escaped. But they poisoned his drink with anarchist imbibings. Darwinian accelerators."

"Transalimentary tinctures!" said Toby, remembering his recovered Academy paper.

She shook with rage. "He became the dragon, the Academy's beast. Forced to work a furnace like a lowly bellows. Wretches! And we have watched each other, beast and beast, across this river, as the brothers have fallen out and fought, and kept us slaves. Until today."

The spider rotated herself, surveying the destruction. Toby smelled a gathering storm. He had put this in motion. He didn't know if he could stop it. He didn't know if he should.

When he could speak again, it was with a waver. "What will happen?"

"There is a new world to create. My fiber can build structures light enough for flight, and my husband designed powerful engines. A new world we will make, lighter than iron and steel! We can build anything, with a few human hands. The Academy will work for us. As subjects. As slaves. As they made ussss."

Toby's dreams evaporated like a droplet on a hot steam pipe. She would destroy everything! This had been wrong, all wrong.

Less than ten feet separated him from the door.

He made it half-way before one of her spike-legs struck, cutting off escape. Toby sprawled headlong, rolling over with pain in his knees to find the spider's red eyes in his face, the bulbous body and all those legs rising above.

"You promised three things," she reminded him.

Toby could easily have forgotten he had agreed to any such

thing, but he knew the spider would not.

"You have given me a voice—" she touched the attempt-at-sabotage pipe protruding from her face with a delicate front leg "—and you have enabled this new beginning. Ride with me. Help me. I need human hands. And I will favor you."

It was hardly a choice. Toby wiggled as her foreleg stabbed him through the shirt collar and hoisted him up behind her head. Mercifully from this vantage, Toby could no longer see her red eyes, but the legs crept creepily in his vision. She moved just like the spiders that used to run at him in his bed at the Grim Maiden.

They were soon scuttling across London Bridge, passing upturned cabs, the horses charred and dead, or missing. One lucky one was swimming in the river. Toby decided in that moment. He would live longer if he did what she asked.

Then, he heard a tinking rattle somewhere below.

"Sorry about the teacup," he said, hoping it would not be held against him.

"It provides vibration modulation," she said.

Toby breathed in relief, short lived. "Where are we going?"

"Birmingham. Manchester. Glasgow. Destroying factories. Then, our carbon age will rise."

Toby noted this as the sort of occupation that distracted adults enough to leave him alone. But ideas of escape, of the future he imagined, were gone.

"Where's the dragon?" he asked, as they passed the splintered, burning remains of two match factories, plumes of gray smoke rising into the soft dawn now breaking on the horizon.

The spider turned at a street corner, following the debris. "Before Birmingham," she said, "will be the Academy. First, the Academy."

More from Charlie Nash

Four original science fiction stories, including the award shortlisted "Dellinger". Available in print and digital.

Seven original fantasy stories with a dark twist, including the multi-award shortlisted slipstream experience "The Ghost of Hephaestus". Available in print and digital.